EVERYWHERE
SAVIORS

FRANK DEWEY STALEY

EVERYWHERE SAVIORS

iUniverse books may be ordered through booksellers or by contacting:

iUniverse
1663 Liberty Drive
Bloomington, IN 47403
www.iuniverse.com
844-349-9409

ISBN: 978-1-6632-4437-6 (sc)
ISBN: 978-1-6632-4438-3 (e)

Print information available on the last page.

iUniverse rev. date: 08/22/2022

To Leni and Kate

And in the end the love you take is
equal to the love you make.
Lennon and McCartney

CHAPTER ONE

When Dobro Temple learned of the cancer cells that had taken up residence in his pancreas, his first thought was of the daughter he had not seen in well over a year. Dobro was from strong family stock long-settled in the Allegheny Highlands of Virginia, and he raised his daughter to grow into a woman capable of looking someone in the eye. Sara was headstrong, but this never bothered her father. Her spine, even as she grew into her teens, was straight as a spear; her handshake was firm.

Dobro's ex-wife, a genuine beauty blessed with long blond hair and dark eyebrows, had run off within eighteen months of giving birth to Sara. Dobro had met her at the party of one of his clients and fell rather quickly and unapologetically in love with her. Mara was what many young women living in Los Angeles aspired to be. She didn't work, as she possessed no real skill with which she could have made a living. Education had never really seemed necessary for Mara. The way she looked and the manner in which she carried herself allowed her to remain in the orbit of the rich and famous. She found that once she made her way into the circles of movers and shakers in and around Hollywood, that she was there to stay.

Dobro knew that his young wife was flighty, that it would be a stretch to assume that she would ever truly settle into what his image of what a proper spouse might be. Mara could be apathetic to the way her actions and words affected those around her, Dobro included. She was a taker far more than a giver, and he saw this, as well. But he was entering his mid-thirties focused like a hungry shark on his career and had never really allowed himself a moment of weakness or spontaneity. Mara threw some sexual voodoo at him, and the rest was history. He loved her and she loved the thought of being married to someone so well-connected with the West Coast glitterati.

He had fallen somewhat accidentally into the role of agent to the stars but had flourished once his career path was made apparent. He was honest and his clients were comforted by his unwavering sense of looking after them. That his young wife ran off with one of his clients, an actor who had just jumped from roles portraying strong silent types to roles portraying strong and slightly-damaged silent types, didn't surprise him as much as it hurt him. Mara, like many of the people he had encountered since taking up residence on the West Coast, had the moral compass of a roulette wheel.

And there was this daughter to raise. The youngest of five children back in Virginia, Dobro had almost no experience in matters such as diapers and doctor appointments. He had gone to Los Angeles to work for an accounting firm which handled much of the tax filings for studios and the directors, actors and crew members employed by them. Two years in, he agreed to help an actress handle an inheritance that out-of-the-blue came her way. She broke her promise to keep the fact that he had helped her on the side between them, and his future was determined. That he was fired came as no shock to him. That word-of-mouth accolades from the actress singing praises for the strong and sensitive way Dobro handled her issue could bring him a string of potential clients so rapidly was a pleasant surprise. Within a year he was earning ten percent of the gross income of five clients. The Dobro Temple Agency was on its way. He trade-marked the name and moved into a rented second floor office suite in Santa Monica. When his lease expired in thirty-six months, he bought the building. It was a red brick, unpretentious two story with dark windows. Situated on a side street not far from the pier, it had no views of the ocean. But it was solid and well-structured and was walking distance to several restaurants and a parking lot loaded with a variety of food trucks. There were palm trees out front.

Dobro was a firm believer in karma; good things happen to good people, and he was certainly near the top of that list. A phone call to a home-help agency which provided *au pairs* to well-off households in Southern California brought immediate results. Of the three women who visited him in his Santa Monica office, Dobro selected Pei Ling to be the daytime care-giver to his young daughter. She was tall and spoke English with some difficulty. Her black hair was pulled back into a ponytail. She had come to America to study medicine at UCLA but had been forced to suspend her education when her father was injured at the Shanghai factory which had employed him his entire adult life. With no money coming from home, she was inches from poverty. But she had no intention of returning. In her mind this would be failure, and failure was not an option. She moved from one job to the next with the only criteria being that the size of the new paycheck be larger than the one it was replacing. She didn't own a car, but that was not important. She had never learned to drive. She lived in a studio apartment on the edge of a truly sketchy neighborhood and walked each day to and from the bus stop.

She lied to Dobro when she told him that she had extensive experience in taking care of children and he knew this. He had an uncanny and very valuable ability to spot dishonesties large and meaningless. But she took pride in the fact that she had never missed a day of school or work, and this offered Dobro a sense of relief. It was not that he couldn't work from home on occasions that Sara could not be cared for by someone else, he simply needed these instances to be as infrequent as possible.

Pei Ling accepted his offer of employment without smiling. She was serious and stoic, as Dobro knew many Asian people to be. But she also possessed a genuine sadness, and this registered with her new employer.

As he looked back at the day-to-day that was life raising Sara, he could only identify the rare occasion or episode that he would have done something differently. He remembered his parents, many years ago and back in Virginia sitting at the kitchen table discussing some no doubt minor transgression one of his older sisters had committed.

"You have your girls," said his father to his wife and to the world in general, "you love them. Then they turn thirteen, and you hate them. Then they turn eighteen or so, and you love them again."

"They come back to you," said his mother.

But Sara had not come back.

The early years were a blend of frustration and magnificence. Dobro and his daughter lived in a small bungalow in Torrance. Before running away, Mara had expressed a strong desire to catch up on the sleep she had lost through the latter stages of her pregnancy, not to mention the delivery. That Dobro agreed to climb out of bed each time their baby daughter needed attention did not surprise Mara. That he did this so silently and efficiently should have warmed her. It did not. She slept away the hours in a cocoon and probably didn't notice.

Pei Ling proved to be a blessing. She rode the bus from her shabby apartment many miles away and showed up on time every morning. She entered the house through the kitchen and often found her employer sitting in a chair opposite his daughter's high-chair. That he spoke in an adult voice to his baby as he fed her with a tiny spoon from a small jar of mush seemed not a bit out of the ordinary. She always offered to take over and let him finish getting ready for work, but this ritual, conducted almost every morning, seemed important to Dobro.

He recognized early on that it would be a game-changer if Pei Ling could drive. Until such time as he could make this happen, he was relegated to leaving his office and driving Sara to this and that appointment. Not that he wished to skirt his way around these responsibilities. He was fully committed as a father and wouldn't have missed a doctor's appointment for anything. But there was always the minutia of raising a child that demanded a quick trip for groceries or diapers. And tending to Sara was not Pei Ling's only task. Dobro had hired her to keep up with the house in addition to that. Although she rarely called him at work with these little emergencies, it was usually a time of noticeable inconvenience when she did.

The Security Driving School was hired on to provide Pei Ling the necessary skills to navigate the roads and highways of Southern California. As a little girl in Shanghai, and of course since moving to Los Angeles, she had witnessed bustling traffic, but never as a participant. The notion of driving a car through the quagmire that was the traffic grid in and around the sprawling collection of cities terrified her. But she was the product of an upbringing that disallowed anything but stoicism and tenacity in the face of challenge. Each morning for a half of an hour before Dobro drove away towards Santa Monica, she climbed into the car that was parked in front. The four-door Volkswagen sedan waiting for her was fitted with a yellow *Student Driver* sign on the roof, and the man sitting in the passenger-side seat was the owner of the company. That these lessons took place every weekday, and that they were so clearly set up as to inconvenience Mr. Temple as little as possible was a bit unusual. But Dobro was very steadily becoming a rich man, and these little accommodations, he was finding, could be arranged for with a phone call and a few extra dollars.

Pei Ling attacked the challenge of learning to drive as if in an anatomy class. She memorized the *Rules of the Road* manual Dobro had picked up for her at the Department of Motor Vehicles office. Once she had earned her Learner's

Permit and could drive legally so long as Dobro was along for the ride, she asked to drive on every occasion a trip was necessary. Occasionally, and usually on a Saturday, Sara would be safely ensconced in her car seat in the back, as Pei Ling and Dobro drove to the supermarket for a week's worth of provisions. That no eyebrows were raised by fellow shoppers as they meandered from aisle to aisle in the store was not surprising. A thirty something year-old man in the company of a twenty year-old Asian woman carrying a blonde-haired infant in a sling across her chest could have raised questions. But this was Southern California and most of the area's inhabitants thought it uncool to take notice of such things.

Not surprisingly, Pei Ling did not miss an answer on her written test. As Dobro sat in the cavernous waiting area of the Department of Motor Vehicles with his daughter bouncing happily on his knee, Pei Ling took her road test. Her judge that Saturday morning was an overweight and extremely unhealthy-looking man named Ramirez.

"You know the reputation you Asian women have on the roads, right?" he asked as she attempted to parallel park.

When her road test had been completed, and after Agent Ramirez had signed off on her ability to operate a motor vehicle safely, Pei Ling's photo was taken, and her new license was minted. That she was the first person in her entire extended family to possess such a thing could have been a milestone. But it was not. When the plastic card was handed to her from across the counter, her demeanor was unchanged.

As she drove her employer and his young daughter away from the Department of Motor Vehicles, Dobro gave her directions to a car lot not far off the path back to Torrance. He held Sara on his knee in the show room lounge as Pei Ling walked from car to car at the Toyota Dealership, and then again as she test-drove the gray, four-door vehicle she had liked.

When Pei Ling and the salesman returned to the lot, Dobro handed over his daughter and walked into the dealership offices to finalize the sale.

"Here you go," he said to Pei Ling as he handed her a set of keys. "Just so we're clear, Pei Ling, I own the car, but you are free to use it in any way you want to. You can drive it home to your apartment and use it any way at all. No more buses."

"Thank you, Mr. Temple," she said. "This is very kind of you."

"Trust me, Pei Ling. This will make life a lot easier for me, too."

They transferred the car seat to Pei Ling's Toyota and the young woman loaded Sara into the back. Dobro was headed to his office to meet with a client. He could not be certain, but he had a good hunch that Pei Ling was smiling as she drove away. This was a first, and the thought of it gave him comfort.

Dobro road along with the real estate agent he had hired to find a larger home when Sara turned five. The bungalow in Torrance had been a suitable place to live, but he needed more space. He had not yet discussed the possibility of Pei Ling moving in with them, but this was on the horizon. His client base had expanded to the point of his having to take on two employees, and his travel schedule was now a genuine concern. Pei Ling had remained dependable; she never balked at his request for her to stay with Sara while he was gone on overnights. But having Pei Ling transition to live-in status would be a relief.

Topanga Canyon was carved into a mountainside just off the Pacific Coast Highway, and it had remained one of the true and last bastions of groovy hipness in America. Men with ponytails and women wearing sun dresses and sandals were common sites at the few meeting places the area had to offer. The homes built along the winding roads were eclectic in their architectural designs. They seemed built as much for privacy as any other amenity, and they lent a certain status to those who owned them. It was a place to live that spoke to one's uniqueness. And the schools attended by children living there were known to be free-thinking and open.

Mary Elizabeth Turner was the owner-agent of a small real estate firm which catered to higher-end buyers and sellers. She was a woman who wore her success comfortably. She was attractive, with slightly graying, shoulder-length hair, piercing blue eyes and a runner's body. The stone in her wedding ring was as large as any Dobro had ever seen.

As she pulled her Cadillac into the twisting driveway beneath the house she had brought Dobro to see, she rattled off a seemingly endless list of positives attached to the place. Schools, of course. A small pool, nice decking, privacy, three bedrooms, three baths, a large kitchen. More privacy.

Dobro had never been one to conform to trends. His criteria for any house he might purchase was value and practicality. That the house was in an area that appealed to free-thinkers, artists, pottery enthusiasts and vegetarians, would not enter into his decision making. He did nothing in his life simply for the sake of image enhancement. Granted, he had enjoyed the wardrobe options that came along with the career change when he was fired from the accounting group and started his agency. He often wore slacks and a dress shirt to his office in Santa Monica. Even on those days when he dressed down, a tee shirt and jeans, he wore high-end dress shoes. Never loafers; always lace-up oxfords. And never with socks. But even his clothing was selected for comfort more than for impressing anyone.

As Dobro walked from room to room with Mary, he made mental notes, visions of a sort. Sara swimming in the pool, Pei Ling standing at the counter in the kitchen preparing dinner, himself sitting on the deck reading or talking with a client on the phone.

"What do you think?" asked Mary.

"I like it," he said. "I like it a lot, actually. It's almost like living in a well-built tree house with all the creature comforts you could ask for."

"Well, I have to tell you that there are several other potentials interested in this place. That's not real estate talk, Mr. Temple. That's the reality."

"What might we be looking at? Price wise, I mean?"

"Well, Mr. Temple, we're living in the nineties. It's most definitely a sellers' market. They're asking eight hundred thou for this place. I know that sounds like a big number, but they're not making any more land in Southern California. This place will be worth well over a million in a few years."

They were standing in the kitchen of what was to be Dobro Temple's new home. It was airy and clean, the afternoon sun providing exactly the right amount of light for the moment to seem staged. He ran the numbers through his head. He again pictured his daughter, this time in the room he knew would be hers.

"Let's offer seven fifty," he said. "What do you think?"

As she drove Dobro back to his office in Santa Monica, she asked him about his daughter, about where he had grown up, about his likes and dislikes. Of note, she did not ask a single question about any of the stars or celebrities his agency might be handling. The degree to which the doctor-patient privilege exists pales in comparison to that governing the agent-client connection. She suspected this and figured it best to avoid uncomfortable conversation.

Thirty minutes after Dobro had returned to his office, he got the call.

"They'll go seven seventy-five," she said.

After a moment of final contemplation, his feet resting on his desk, Dobro nodded.

"Can you bring the paperwork to my office, Mary?"

It took just under eleven minutes to talk Pei Ling into moving in with them. Dobro pointed out that his schedule was not going to get any lighter, that the drive from Pei Ling's apartment was not going to get any shorter, that the young woman's financial picture could most certainly become brighter.

"I'll pay you the same, Pei Ling. With the money you save from not paying rent, you can do whatever you want. And we'll work something out so that you can have a couple of vacations each year. Maybe visit your family."

"It's a big step," she said.

"You could go back to school," said Dobro. "Sara starts the first grade next year. You could drop her at school and shoot into town, take a couple classes and be back in time to pick her up. It might be perfect, Pei Ling."

The young woman smiled and began to cry. These reactions happened in an instant. They had been waiting to come out since her father's injury forced her to abandon her education. Her hand went to her face in a futile effort to hide her tears. Droplets of salt water seeped through her fingers and ran down her wrist.

When she had composed herself and wiped one last time across her eyes and cheeks with the back of her hand, she looked directly at her employer. Her eyes were red but possessed a brightness a bit like sunlight through red glass.

"You're the nicest person I've ever met, Mr. Temple."

"I really think it's time you started calling me Dobro," he said.

Despite this invitation, she never did.

Dobro had always processed his world through numbers. An excellent student, he shone brightly in all of his math classes as a boy. Although tempted to follow a path towards academia, he listened to the wise advice of his parents and earned his degree in accounting. People always needed accountants they had told him.

Numbers were a language in and of themselves to Dobro, and as he sat in his office or on his deck processing them, they made sense. When Sara started the first grade Pei Ling returned to school; when Sara started the fourth grade Pei Ling would have earned her Bachelors' Degree; when Sara entered the eighth grade Pei Ling would be knee-deep in medical school; Sara would be graduating from high school when Pei Ling was fully entrenched in her residency.

Although fluid, this timeline made all the sense in the world to Dobro. It spoke to him and validated the decisions he had made and the developments he had put into motion.

Life is often what happens when we are making plans, but Dobro's world stayed relatively on course. With an all but unfathomable amount of help from Pei Ling, he went through the weeks, months and years of his life raising his daughter to be strong and filled with confidence. But early on, as Sara entered those tumultuous years of pre-teen challenges, Dobro had had to focus on balance.

The combined work ethic on display between himself and Pei Ling would have steered a Mennonite dairy farmer towards greater effort. There was downtime, of course, but never once, not for an instant, while there remained some task to complete, some work lingering on the horizon. Sara saw this and drank it in. She applied herself diligently to schoolwork, to soccer, to dance class, to the swim team. She was bright, and she possessed a charming wittiness that made her father smile, and that made Pei Ling purse her lips.

But there were Yin and Yang concepts at play in Sara's life. This was Southern California after all, and there were influences that attempted to seep into her consciousness that lay in opposition to the lessons learned from her father and Pei Ling. Although the free-spirit movement of the 60's had long-since come and gone, the children raised by this generation had grown up with much the same apathy towards conventional wisdom and lifestyle choices. Life, for many of the children Sara went to school with, was not to be infected with concepts of planning, hard work and practicality. Although clearly incapable of enumerating these concepts, many of these kids felt them. Surfing was good; studying was a necessary evil.

And there were other and as equally potent influences at play in the growth and emotional development of Dobro's daughter. Not often, but occasionally, a client of Dobro's would visit the house in Topanga for some quality time, some guidance, some understanding or encouragement. Sara's was an inquisitive nature both genetically and by virtue of the way she had been raised. She knew better than to eavesdrop on these occasions, but the allure of gleaning bits and pieces of the lives of the celebrities she knew her father handled drew her in like a moth to flame. She sat on the periphery of these conversations, a book on her lap, a serious look on her young face, and listened intently to the problems and predicaments faced by the rich and famous.

As she aged, the ruse of not listening became less and less necessary. There were events she attended with her father. Holiday open house affairs at his office in Santa Monica or in some hotel banquet hall. As Sara moved fully through her teenage years, she was introduced regularly to the artists, actors, musicians and writers represented by her father. It was a wide swath of people, problems and lifestyles to which she was introduced, but the variety was condensed into the spectrum that held only the truly creative. Creativity always comes at a price, and it is almost always fragility. She saw it all.

She inherited her work ethic from her father, and it was most certainly more deeply developed in her, the result of watching the stoic and serious Pei Ling. Although she had never known her mother, a maturing Sara Temple could only assume that the ease with which she connected with people, that the efforts everyone around her seemed always willing to make to get to know her, that these qualities were gifts from her mother. She had seen pictures of a young Mara, discovered one afternoon when she had just turned thirteen and thought it justified to snoop in the drawers of her father's desk. She thought the young woman in the photos to be prettier than she herself was, of course more exotic and mysterious. But she stared for many moments at the photos in an effort to detect a hint of emotion that might be painted on her mother's face. She saw the sizzle in her mother's attitude and in the marginally provocative poses; but to her way of thinking, there was no substance.

Betty Bonzo filled every room she ever entered with substance. When she made her appearance at a holiday gathering hosted by The Dobro Temple Agency, those enjoying themselves sipping champagne and mingling at the upscale West Hollywood hotel Dobro had reserved for the occasion felt her arrival more than saw it.

"Who's that?" Sara asked her father.

Now sixteen, just, Sara had been allowed to accompany her father for the first time to one of his larger events, this particular one in late May. One of Dobro's strong selling points to potential clients was the family element of his agency, and Sara's presence was a demonstration of this. This was not marketing coming from him. He became genuinely attached to the people he represented. He worked tirelessly to put them in good positions, and not just financially. He cared to a fault.

"That's Betty Bonzo. I believe she's here as someone's guest. I didn't see who she came in with."

"No. I mean, who is she? What does she do?"

"She's a singer-songwriter," said Dobro to his daughter who seemed incapable of looking away from the subject of their discussion. "She's in a band. Have you heard of Women With No Feet?"

Sara's laugh ended in a groan.

"That's not the name of a real band is it, dad?"

"It is. They're very indy and loud," he said. "I really haven't listened to very much of their work, to be honest. Oh, there's her date."

Sara turned her attention to the entrance and saw an older woman dressed as if for the opera. She was tall and thin, her snow-white hair pulled up tight to the top her head, and she wore a sparkling necklace that bordered on ostentation. One more red gemstone would have been too many. Her black dress was floor-length, and a white wrap made from the fur of some small animal covered her shoulders.

"That's Margo Malone," said Dobro to his daughter. "She's a record producer and is one of my clients. Has been for a long time. A really nice woman. C'mon, let's go say hello."

As they approached their newest guests to greet them, Sara catalogued Betty Bonzo's appearance. Dark slacks and matching jacket that seemed more suited to a bank officer than a rock star, light brown hair cut short enough to point in all directions, a pair of sandals with no socks. Whatever steps Betty Bonzo had taken to prepare herself for this gathering, cleaning her toenails was not among them. She was different from anyone Sara had ever encountered, with a countenance of allure and disgust in equal portions. She had not bothered to add a shirt of any kind under the jacket, and her breasts were barely unexposed.

"Aloha, Dobro," said Margo. "Thanks ever so much for inviting me again this year. I just love these little gatherings."

"And it's my greatest pleasure to have you join us, Margo. You know, we've been together for over ten years? Who does that in our business anymore?"

"It's because you're genuine, Dobro. You're a real person. And who might this be?" she asked adjusting her line of sight to Sara.

"Margo, this is my daughter Sara. I thought it was high time some of my client family meet my real family."

"Delighted," said Margo.

Sara started to extend her hand but stopped when it was obvious that Margo had no intention of accepting it. Betty Bonzo reached quickly across the front of her elegant date's body and clasped Sara's hand firmly.

"I'm Betty," she said. "Nice to meet you, Sara. And you must be the Dobro that Margo is always going on and on about."

"A pleasure," he said as Betty exchanged Sara's hand for his. "I'm so glad you could join us."

"What do you do?" asked Betty.

This was an hour later, and she sat in a corner of the expansive, nicely-decorated room chatting with Sara.

"I go to high school," said Sara.

"No, I mean for fun. What do you do to flirt around the edges of anarchy kind of stuff?"

"That sounds like a line in a song," said Sara. "I don't know. Usual stuff. I like to take ski trips with my friends, go to the beach. That kind of thing."

"Pretty wild, Sara," said Betty with a wide grin. "If I could offer you some advice, I'd tell you to try to do something crazy once in a while."

Sara wanted to ask for a list of examples but thought this would be too obvious an indication of her naivete. And she couldn't stop staring at Betty's feet.

"What's up with my feet?" she asked. "You keep staring at them."

Sara blushed instantly and thought she could feel perspiration on her upper lip.

"Sorry, I just like your sandals," she said.

"I think you like my feet," said Betty. "And God, but I could use a foot rub right about now."

Sara looked away.

"Who's Margo?" asked Sara in an obvious attempt to change the subject.

"She's sort of my spiritual guide and mentor. She has a record label," said Betty. "It's alright about my feet. We're just two chicks sitting here talking, Sara. Haven't you noticed? We're sitting here in a little cloud of honesty. There's something really cool about that, isn't there?"

Sara nodded.

"What kind of music do you do? I'm really sorry that I haven't heard anything you've done...I'm going to get some of your music the next time I'm out...but what's it like?"

"It's loud," said Betty.

"That's what my father said. What's it about?"

"Mostly the female anatomy. We're all kind of dyke-ish, all the members of the band. So, we write a lot of stuff about eating pussy, doing it with girls, that kind of thing. We've been told that our music is very niche. Whatever the fuck that means."

"That sounds interesting," said Sara.

"Does it really, Sara? Or are you just saying that? If it really does sound interesting to you, you should come and hang out with me some Saturday, some day you're not in school."

Sara was taken aback by the openness with which Betty spoke. She wondered if the lack of any noticeable filter was because Betty was talking to a high school girl, if her pronouncements would have been more circumspect if a full-on adult had joined the conversation. Was the singer-songwriter just showing off?

"It does sound interesting," she said after a small hesitation. "I'm not sure I'm all that interested in some of the activities you just mentioned…I'm just not sure about any of that, but I think I would enjoy spending some time with you. Dad has had a couple of people, his clients, up to the house for dinner a few times. One was an actor; another guy wrote scripts for television shows. I find you creative types to be very interesting."

"Is that what I am?" said Betty with a bright smile. "A creative type? Maybe we'll change the name of the band to The Creative Types. That might work."

"I didn't mean to typecast you," said Sara. She was not shrinking into herself as she said this. Her eyes did not move from Betty's. She was holding her ground as one would not expect a sixteen year-old girl to be able to. "As someone who has very little creativity, at least in the world of music, I think it would be fun to get to know someone like you. Not someone who's your *type*, but someone like you *specifically.*"

Betty took a business card out of the left pocket of her black trousers and handed it to Sara.

"Here's my number, girl. Give me a call sometime and we can hang out. We can talk all night about creativity. And you could stare at my feet all you want to."

Betty smiled again, shook Sara's hand and went to find Margo.

Sara didn't call her for a couple weeks. She wanted to call the day after meeting Betty Bonzo, but decided to wait out of some unwritten, I-don't-want-to-appear-needy friendship decorum. Sara was also not totally certain as to what her expectations were. Betty was fascinating to her, that much was clear. She had enjoyed their chat; Betty's use of earthy language was more unique than just simply naughty in Sara's mind. And the insights she gleaned were just the stuff a sixteen tear-old, independent girl born and raised in upper-crust Southern California would find to be profound. Sara had experimented with minor sexual activities with both boys and girls, but that was not what it was about with Betty. Betty was a lifestyle more than an interesting person, and Sara wanted to be around more of it. That said, since the evening they met, Sara could not get the image of Betty's feet out of her mind.

"Of course, I remember you. You're the agent's daughter," Betty said into the phone.

"That's me. I just kind of stumbled on the card you gave me and thought I'd give you a call," said Sara.

"I'm glad you did. So, how's high school going? Dating all those surfer boys?"

"No. I actually prefer to hang out with my friends than do the whole dating thing. It's usually awkward and the expectations are never what the actual date turns out to be."

"You just haven't met the right date, Sara. Trust me, when you do, you'll throw all those friends out the fucking window. So, what are you up to?"

Sara was sitting at the desk in her bedroom. She wore a two-piece swimsuit that had been a gift from Pei Ling on her sixteenth birthday. The print of the fabric was french fries floating in a sea of yellow. It was just quirky enough for Sara to think it cool.

"Not much. We're wrapping up the school year, so there's lots of studying for tests. The usual stuff with my friends. I'm about to go for a swim actually."

"Why did you call me, Sara?"

This question took the young woman aback. She sat up in her chair and tilted her head as if looking somewhere in her brain for an answer.

"I'm really not sure," she said after a brief hesitation. "I mean, you gave me your card, so I kind of thought you might *want* me to call you. Other than that, I liked talking to you at my dad's party the other night. I thought you were interesting, and that maybe I'd like to have a conversation with you again."

"You really just want to stare at my feet again, don't you?" said Betty with a laugh.

Sara smiled widely.

"For the last f-ing time, Betty, I just liked your sandals."

They met the following Saturday at a juice bar. Sara arrived early and took a seat at one of the outside tables. She sat looking into the sunlight as a courtesy to Betty. When asked if she'd like to order she declined.

Betty showed up ten minutes late and did not apologize. She wore faded jeans that rode low on her hips and a sleeveless, psychedelic-print tee shirt that left a portion of her stomach exposed. She carried a large cotton bag over her shoulder. The sandals Sara remembered from the night they met completed the ensemble; Betty's toenails were chipped and uneven, grayish dirt under each of them.

Sara stood as Betty approached the table. Betty dropped her bag and took Sara's hands into her own. She kissed the young woman quickly on the mouth and sat in the seat that positioned her back to the sun.

"It's really good to see you, Sara. I'm glad you called me."

"Me too," said Sara. "I thought about it a while ago, but I've been kind of busy wrapping up the school year."

"What grade are you in?"

"I'm going into my senior year next year. Where did you go to high school? Where are you from, Betty?"

"New York. Long Island, actually. I came out here right after high school and started hanging out with some indy musicians. I played the guitar a little back then, but I was pretty shitty. But I worked at it, met some people that helped me, hooked up with some other girls who wanted to put out the same kind of music as me. And then we just kind of made it, you know? We played a lot of tiny clubs, and we were really enjoying it. And then, all of a sudden, we get signed by a label. Who could have ever guessed it, right?"

"I listened to a couple of your albums," said Sara.

A waitress appeared with note pad and pencil in hand. She was extremely tall and was dressed as if to play a tennis match: her shorts, the collared shirt and her shoes and socks were all blindingly white.

"Oh, hi," said Betty to the waitress. "Jesus, can you turn that outfit down a little? I left my sunglasses in the car."

The woman smiled.

"Good afternoon, ladies. My name's Echo, and I'll be serving you today. Can we start out with something to drink?"

"We're at a juice bar," said Betty. "I'm guessing the chances that we're going to have something to drink are pretty good, right, Echo?"

Betty ordered a frappe made with multiple fruits and vegetables. Sara went with a mango and strawberry shake.

"What'd you think of the music?" Betty asked after their waitress had gone to fetch their drinks.

"You were right. It's loud. But I liked it. I liked a lot of your lyrics."

"Which lyrics?" asked Betty.

"I don't know. A lot of the songs deal with the fact that you, as a woman, don't need the conventional relationships that we all seem to think are so necessary. That song about not needing a dick to make your life complete, I liked that. And the one about nuking the sperm whales, that was funny. I guess I like the irreverence."

"That would be us," said Betty Bonzo. "We are some irreverent bitches, Sara."

Sara wanted desperately to drop something, giving her a chance to look at Betty's feet. She had no explanation for the odd allure, but she couldn't deny it. She had never been around anyone as earthy, and she was enjoying the aura Betty gave off. She noted the hair under Betty Bonzo's armpits, the short and unruly hair on her head that she would have guessed had not been washed in days, the clothing that was intended to impress absolutely no one. The other adult women that Sara had been exposed to were proper. Teachers, professional types that she had met through her father, certainly Pei Ling, all put themselves together with a properness that Betty obviously did not care about. Sara was basking in the differentness as she sat looking into the sun over Betty's exposed shoulder.

The tall woman delivered their drinks with a flourish, repeating what they ordered as she placed the large glasses in front of them.

"What kind of name is Echo?" asked Betty.

"My parents were real flower children," she said. "It has something to do with being on the same plane, being able to experience the same exact thing as someone else. At least that's my understanding of it. To be honest, I just roll with it."

"It's a cool name," said Sara. "I like it."

"I think it's a stupid fucking name," said Betty after the waitress had left. "And all the white clothes. I feel like I'm in a sanitarium or something. How's your drink?"

"It's good. Where did you get the name Bonzo?"

Betty reached across the table and took Sara's drink. She used the straw Sara had been using and took a large taste before sliding the glass back.

"That's really good," she said. "I just picked the name one night when we were smoking a lot of dope and we were watching television. That stupid kid's show was on, the one with the clown, Bozo, so I just altered it a little. It just seemed to work."

"What was your last name before that?" asked Sara as she sipped her drink.

"Horowitz. Elizabeth Rachel Horowitz. Great name for an irreverent rock star, right, Sara?"

"Where are you parked?" asked Betty as they left the juice bar.

"Over there," said Sara pointing to the far end of the lot.

"I'll walk you to your car," said Betty.

Betty kissed her again as they stood beside the car Sara's father had presented to her on her sixteenth birthday, this time allowing their lips to stay together just slightly longer.

"You ever been with a woman, Sara?"

"Not really. Kind of."

"You're going to have to explain to me one of these days what *kind of* means."

Sara smiled.

"Call me again if it's something you want to do, okay? We could get another fancy drink from Echo or something."

"I will," said Sara as she slipped into her car. "I'll call you for sure."

"Did you have a good afternoon?"

This was Pei Ling standing at the island countertop in the middle of the kitchen. As Sara had moved from grade to grade in high school, Pei Ling had spent less and less time at the house in Topanga. She had moved into a small but comfortable apartment within a few miles of campus, and only spent nights at the house when Dobro was away on business. This arrangement did not bother Sara as it would have many young people her age. Having Pei Ling around on those nights gave her father comfort. She saw this and it pleased her. Pei Ling had retained her room at the house even after she moved out and was conspicuously out of Sara's hair. She showed up three times a week to clean the place, and on those evenings, she prepared dinner. This happened to be a cleaning day.

"It was nice," said Sara dropping her keys into a red ceramic bowl placed on a table near the entry to the kitchen. "What're you cooking?"

"What it seems like I always cook," said Pei Ling. "Stir fry. Your father loves stir fry. I think it's because I'm Chinese that he likes it so much. He thinks I add some magic Chinese spice to it."

"How's school?" asked Sara as she took a seat on one of the stools facing the countertop.

"I have to think about residency now," said Pei Ling. "I have options, but I need to talk to your father. It will mean that I probably won't be able to spend very much time here. Even on weekends."

"You don't need to worry about it, Pei Ling. You're family. Dad looks at you as if you're a member of our tight, little nuclear unit. He'll completely understand. He's very proud of you, you know? And, trust me, I'm certainly old enough now that I don't need a sitter for the nights he's away."

Pei Ling stopped chopping the celery stalks that were on the cutting board in front of her. Through all the years, her hair style had not changed. Long on the sides and in the back, cut into bangs in the front. As a little girl, Sara had derived great pleasure from playing with Pei Ling's hair. Brushes, barrettes, hair clips. And Pei Ling, the stoic and strong woman from whom Sara had learned so much, had simply sat and allowed the little girl to play hairdresser.

"How does that look?" an eight year-old Sara would ask, holding a mirror up for her pretend client to peek at.

"Gosh, it's so special. However do you do that?"

And they would laugh. And in as genuine display of love as could possibly be imagined, Pei Ling would leave her hair as Sara had created it until Dobro Temple returned from work and the three of them sat eating their dinner.

"I like what you've done to your hair," Dobro would often say.

"Thank you, Mr. Temple. I went to the hairdresser today."

Pei Ling took a long look at Sara before returning to her chopping. For all intents and purposes, the two women had grown up together. Pei Ling was often silent, making great effort to keep her feelings to herself. But Sara was that special combination of empathy and tenacity that seemed always to break through the defenses. Pei Ling's longer-than-usual bangs fell over the front of her face as might a curtain; Sara could see through them as if the light making its way to her could bend and curve on its journey through the black hair.

Sara was rarely silent. She spoke openly and freely of her experiences, her complaints, her wins and losses. But on those occasions when she was silent, when there seemed something of substance under the surface, Pei Ling had the key to unlock what was important and what was trivial. She knew every subtle nuance of Sara's body language, the way she sat, the way she refused to lose eye contact when they spoke, the manner in which she used her hands to make a point. She could read Sara like tea leaves and knew when secrets were there for the finding.

"What did you this afternoon that was so much fun?"

"Not much," said Sara. "I met a new friend at a juice bar. The one over by that Italian restaurant that dad always takes us to."

"Who's the new friend?" asked Pei Ling without looking up from her cutting board.

"It's actually a musician that I met a couple weeks ago at one of dad's little gatherings. It's not his client. She was there with her agent...a client of dad's."

"So, she's not a student? She doesn't go to your school?"

"No. She's older. A little younger than you."

Pei Ling smiled.

"Well, if she's younger than me, I'm sure she's alright."

"She's fun," said Sara. "Quite a mouth on her, but interesting. I'll be back."

Sara left the kitchen and headed to her room, closing the door behind her. She picked up the CD case holding the latest album produced by her newest friend and lay on her bed looking at the picture of the band on the back cover. She thought of what Betty Bonzo might be doing just then. She wondered if the opportunity would ever present itself that Betty would visit her at her house, swim in her pool, sit chatting in her kitchen.

She rose and slipped out of her clothing, put on the yellow french fry swimsuit and padded, barefoot, to the sliding door that opened to the deck and pool.

"What time's dinner?" she asked Pei Ling as she crossed the wood floor on her way out.

"About seven. Just like always."

Pei Ling had filled separate bowls with the variety of vegetables she had just chopped and covered them with plastic wrap. She took a package of chicken breasts out of the refrigerator and began to remove the white paper. She stopped and looked out to the deck just as Sara was jumping into the deep end of the small pool. She saw Sara's blond hair float on the surface as she lingered under the water for a few moments.

Pei Ling did not know what the significance of Sara's new friend was, but she was certain that there was something there, something Sara had not wanted to share or even hint at. It wasn't that she didn't trust musicians, artists or actors, it was simply that she knew nothing of their world. Pei Ling was practical; every action in her life created a reaction, and she was unsettled at not being able to predict these reactions. She didn't worry for Sara at this point as much as she was merely frustrated at not having enough information to predict the future. And she knew that she would not share her concern, this nagging nibble at her heart, with Dobro Temple. Pei Ling had earned Sara's trust over these years by keeping things to herself. At least the little things. And she was hopeful that this was just another little thing, the kind of development that happens to young women moving from one stage of adult experiences to another.

Betty Bonzo arrived late to their next meeting. It was at the same juice bar, and Sara sat in the same seat as she waited. Betty was unapologetic when she arrived. Before sitting, she bent at the waist and kissed Sara on the mouth.

"Here," she said," as she handed Sara a box. "I got you a pair of sandals just like mine. Now we're twins. And you don't have to stare at my feet anymore."

Sara felt herself blushing, more from being kissed by a woman in public than from receiving Betty's gift. It unsettled her, but she enjoyed the warmth that seemed to radiate throughout her body.

"Thank you, Betty. That's very sweet of you. I'll wear them all the time."

"I can't remember the last time anyone referred to me as sweet," said Betty as she took her seat.

Sara removed her new sandals from the box.

"I'm going to wear them now," she said as she slipped out of her shoes and strapped the sandals on. "What do you think?"

"I think we're going to have to get you some shabby clothes and then make you a member of the band," said Betty.

"I can't play any instruments," said Sara.

"Believe me, baby, a lot of people say that about us already."

They ordered drinks and sat chatting for close to an hour. Sara talked about school, and Betty seemed genuinely interested.

"Boys are just penises at your age, walking around, bumping into anything they can possibly bump into. And I'd like to tell you that they change, that they develop any kind of sense of proportion when they get older. But for the most part, they don't. I wish more of them were gay so that they'd leave us alone."

"They're not all that way," said Sara. "Some of the boys I know, some of my friends, they're very cool people."

"They're the minority," said Betty. "Most of them just want to get in your pants."

"You sound a little jaded," said Sara. "There have got to be men in your life that you respect, right? I mean, not every single one of them is crap, like you're saying."

"You a virgin, Sara?"

Again, Sara felt herself warming from within. She knew her cheeks were burning but could do absolutely nothing about it.

"No," she whispered. "But I only did it one time. A few months ago, with this boy I was dating pretty seriously."

"Was he different after he did you than he was before?"

Sara thought about this as she sipped her shake. She made a strange face, mouth pursed, brow furrowed.

"He was, I guess. At least a little. But it wasn't like he was just a nice guy until I let him. We've stayed friends."

"So, he's not your boyfriend anymore?"

"No."

"I rest my case," said Betty. "They're all shitheads. Just some of them hide it better."

They drove separately to Betty's apartment after leaving the juice bar. There was not a need for pretense.

"I want you to see my place," said Betty as she handed a credit card to the waiter at the juice bar. "It's really nothing special. I just want you to see it."

As she followed Betty's car, a compact Volkswagen with a convertible top, Sara wondered what she was getting herself into. There was no sense of danger in visiting Betty, but a strong feeling of trepidation wouldn't go away. Betty didn't frighten her, but this situation was most certainly one she had never found herself walking, driving, into. "Just go with it," she said to herself, "what's the worst that can happen."

Betty Bonzo's apartment was less impressive than Sara thought it would be. She was not sure what to expect from a rock star's place, but she was slightly let down at entering Betty's one bedroom, third story walk-up. They had passed the community pool as they walked from the lot to the stairs. It needed skimming and seemed to be filled with a different variant of water than the pool at Sara's home in Topanga. The color was closer to green than blue.

The apartment was dark and had a slight odor of dust and dried leaves. There were unwashed dishes in the sink, and items of clothing had been tossed on most of the furniture. The walls were covered with posters of bands Sara did not recognize, the common denominator of the band mates being dark leather clothing and fierce demeanors.

"Sit," said Betty as she motioned to a table and two chairs just off the kitchenette. "Want a glass of wine?"

Sara had sat in her own kitchen many times listening to her father relate the catastrophic impact drugs and alcohol were capable of producing. He saw it up close and personal. Clients whose careers were destroyed; families broken into pieces incapable of being glued back again. He had said that there was nothing wrong with people having a drink now and then, but that they should think before doing so.

"I'd love a glass of wine," Sara heard herself saying. "But just a small one. I'm driving."

Betty filled two wine glasses from a bottle in the refrigerator. She placed them on the table, the larger one in front of Sara, and sat opposite her.

"Pretty unpretentious, right?" said Betty.

"What do you mean?" asked Sara as she sipped from her glass. "This is good. What is it?"

"Chardonnay," said Betty. "It's all I drink anymore. I used to get after it. Bourbon, vodka, whatever could get me stupid. But that was in a more self-destructive stage. Now I just drink this and smoke a little weed. I meant my apartment. Pretty unpretentious, isn't it?"

"It's nice. It feels comfortable. I expected to see a bunch of guitars all over the place."

"I have one in the bedroom, but the rest of them are at a studio we use to practice and record. I'm afraid of getting broken into here. If that ever happens, they can just take all this useless shit I have laying around and I won't be bothered. I'd probably just walk away and move to a new place."

"That's pretty Zen," said Sara before she could stop herself. She had heard that expression used and was somewhat certain it referred to a laid-back attitude. She sipped her wine again and hoped that Betty Bonzo would not invite her to expand upon the statement.

"What does that really mean?" asked Betty. "I mean, I hear that shit all the time. But what does it really mean? Do you know?"

Sara smiled.

"Not really," she said. "I know it's a philosophical thing, kind of a religious thing that has something to do with

33

Buddhism. But other than just being cool about stuff, no, I really don't know what it means. I was trying to impress you."

Betty stood and stepped to a spot beside Sara's chair. She leaned and kissed her, this time with an open mouth. Sara tasted wine but was unsure whose tongue she was getting it from.

"Do you have any idea how cute you are?" asked Betty.

"I'm not sure I want to be *cute,*" said Sara. "Maybe attractive. Handsome in a womanly sort of way? I'm not sure about *cute.*"

Betty kissed her again, this time more forcefully. Sara could feel her neck strain as she attempted to match the pressure of Betty's mouth pressing into her.

"No," said Betty in almost a whisper. "Cute is good. Cute is just what I need right now. Want to see where I keep my guitar?"

Sara sipped at her wine as Betty stood over her.

"I'm a little wobbly," she said. "I'm not absolutely sure what I want right now. I think I want to go in there with you, but I'm just…I'm just a little nervous. I'm very nervous."

Betty stepped away and removed her shirt. She was not wearing a bra. She placed her hand gently on Sara's cheek and cupped her jawline.

"Please don't be nervous," she said. "Nothing is going to happen that you don't want to happen. We could just lie down and be close if you want to. Just don't be nervous. Don't be *wobbly.*"

This made Sara smile. She stood and let Betty take her hand, leading her through the living room and into her bedroom.

"There's my guitar," she said as she took Sara into her arms. It was the first full-on hug they had shared with each other. Baby kisses in public were nothing to raise eyebrows. But this was a display of purer emotion and physicality. It would not have played in public, even in the year 2001, even in Los Angeles.

"I'm sorry I couldn't, you know, reciprocate," said Sara as she dressed to leave several minutes later.

"Don't be," said Betty. "Lots of girls think they're on the team until it's their turn to go down on someone. That kind of clarifies it for them. But don't worry. That was fun. We're just who we are, you and me. Maybe next time."

Sara allowed Betty to kiss her once more before saying good-bye and leaving. As she drove towards Topanga, she looked at herself repeatedly in the rear view mirror. Her lips were swollen from Betty's forceful kissing. She did not smile as she focused on the road ahead. She played no music and tried to empty her mind. She wanted to slip into a state of Zen but had no idea how to go about doing that.

Pei Ling sat in the window of the living room looking out over the deck and the canyon beyond. This was not one of her regular days to clean or cook; she had come to discuss the future, her future, with her friend and employer Dobro Temple.

"Oh, hi," said Sara as she dropped her keys in the red bowl and went to a cupboard to get a glass. "I didn't think this was one of your days here."

"It isn't," said Pei Ling as she placed the book she was reading face down on her lap. "I need to speak to your father about something."

"You quitting us, Pei Ling?"

"I'm not looking forward to having this conversation with your father, but yes, I have to make some decisions with my career. I'm very sad about it, Sara."

Sara filled her glass with cold water from the tap and joined Pei Ling in the living room. She sat sideways in the matching easy chair, throwing her legs over the arm.

"Sara, are you alright?" asked Pei Ling.

"Yeah, why?"

"Your mouth. You look swollen. You look as if you've been in a fight or something."

"It wasn't a fight, trust me," said Sara with an impish grin.

Pei Ling was silent. She had walked gently on this ground since Sara entered puberty, not fully comfortable in her role as part-time surrogate mother-figure, but well aware that providing guidance to the girl seemingly speeding into womanhood was part of what was expected of her. She had talked to Sara's father on more than one occasion about the level of involvement he wanted her to have in these matters, and he always expressed support and gratitude for what she did.

"Some of these conversations are damn near impossible for me to have with her," he had said. "Forget the fact that they're uncomfortable, some of the details…I'm not even sure I know what I'm talking about."

Pei Ling had approached these discussions with a young Sara Temple as she would a medical examination. The conversations were thorough; all of the girl's questions were answered in detail; the mood in the room remained clinical, almost professional until the subject matter changed to schoolwork and trips to the beach.

Sara was sixteen years old, and Pei Ling, despite never having gone through any real period of sexual experimentation of her own, could only go so far towards understanding Sara's mindset. Hormones are hormones on whatever continent sixteen year-olds play. But Pei Ling's young womanhood had been structured; the codes of ethics and behavior were ingrained. She had started college at the age of seventeen and had never truly made the time for boys. After the injury to her father, when she had been forced to delay her education, her life was consumed with taking care of Sara. Even when Pei Ling returned to school, there seemed few opportunities for sexual expression of any kind. By then, she was older than most of her fellow students. After classes ended each day, there still remained a child for her to raise. And now, in her early thirties, she spoke to Sara more as a medical professional than a woman blessed with genuine knowledge of these things.

"Just promise me that you're being careful, will you please? Just promise me that when you get a boyfriend that you'll practice safe sex, okay?" she said.

"I made you that promise the last time we talked about all of this. On me birthday. Remember?"

"Whatever are you going to do without me?" said Pei Ling with a wide smile.

"Go crazy and get knocked up, I guess," said Sara.

When Dobro Temple arrived home from work, he looked quizzically at Pei Ling. She had not moved from her chair. Sara had changed into the french fry bathing suit, had gone for a swim and was now lying on her back on a towel on the deck.

"What are you doing here, Pei Ling," he asked. "You quitting us?"

His agency had flourished in the last several years. The business, the list of clients, had grown to the point of consuming more of his time than he was willing to give. He'd hired one more agent to help with the workload and had made the decision that this was enough. The business was big enough. He needed nor wanted any more people to represent.

And he knew that in some genuine way Pei Ling was to some degree responsible for this. For the money he made, which was significant; for the lifestyle he lived and was able to raise his daughter in; for the future he had secured for all of them. Her unwavering commitment to his daughter and to him was one of the main building blocks for all of this, and he knew this. He also knew that this day was coming. He and Pei Ling had spoken of it as she moved her way through medical school. But he was unprepared for it on this evening. He knew that when people proclaimed themselves to be ready for a life-change, they often are not. They often have no choice in the matter, and this was Dobro Temple at this moment.

They drove separately to the Italian restaurant Dobro loved. He was known by name and face at many of the upscale dining establishments in and around Los Angeles… it was the rare occasion when he didn't meet some client or business contact for lunch…but he enjoyed the coziness of this place. And the food was delicious.

"So, residency next?"

"Yes," said Pei Ling. "I have a few options, but I'm thinking of staying near here."

"Well, wherever you decide to go, you'll do well," said Dobro. "I can only imagine how proud your parents must be. Doctor Pei Ling Chang."

Pei Lind nodded as she chewed a bite of fresh bread. Her every move seemed always to be delicate.

"I think I'll go see them before I start. I have a little break now, for about a month."

"Why don't we have Angelica set that up for you? Call the office in the morning and give her the dates. She'll take care of it."

"You've done too much already," said Pei Ling.

And he had. Over the course of each of the past several years Dobro had directed his assistant to purchase plane tickets for Pei Ling to visit her family in Shanghai. When Sara was still young, he had had to arrange for a temporary replacement to watch over things while Pei Ling was away. This was an inconvenience, but a minor one. Pei Ling was family and sacrifices always seemed less a bother when family was concerned.

"It's the least we can do," said Dobro closing the door on the subject.

"What's it like when you go home, Pei Ling," asked Sara. "What do you do when you're there?"

"I run a million errands for my parents and for my grandmother. I think they save them up for me."

"Is it as crowded and busy at it looks on television in Shanghai?"

"Worse. So many millions of people. I don't even keep track of how many anymore," said Pei Ling.

"I can't imagine how much you've missed your family all this time," said Sara. "It's had to have been really hard on you."

"And on them," said Dobro without looking up from his salad.

"Why don't you come with me," said Pei Ling to Sara. "Why don't you come visit China with me? If that would be okay with your father, of course."

Dobro looked up, a quizzical look on his face. He was calculating a variety of scenarios, running the trip from start to finish through his brain.

"I think that would be alright," he said. "As long as your parents wouldn't mind."

"They would love to have you, Sara. They have heard me talk so much about you."

Sara broke off a small piece of bread from the loaf resting in a basket in the center of the table. She dipped it in the olive oil her father had poured into the center of a plate. She looked out the large window at the front of the restaurant. She could see people sitting at the outdoor tables of the juice bar she had met Betty Bonzo at. She thought of Betty's near-forcefulness when they had been together in bed. She remembered the swollen and sensitive lips Betty's kisses had left her with.

"That's a sweet offer, Pei Ling, but I think I want to stay home this Summer. I kind of have some plans."

She took the piece of bread into her mouth and chewed with her lips slightly separated. She had quite likely just disappointed two of the three most important people in her life and this bothered her less than she thought it should have.

She realized, almost exactly one week from the night they had all enjoyed dinner out, that she should have decided to go with Pei Ling. It wasn't the trip. Her father was a rich man. She knew this, and also knew that if she really wanted to travel somewhere, that it was within his means to send her. It was that she had based this decision, turning down this wonderful offer to see an exotic place and to spend time with the woman who she could only describe as a mother figure, on an infatuation with someone she rather quickly was losing interest in. She knew that she could still make the trip, that a phone call to her father would roll Angelica into action and plane tickets and such would be arranged. But this would scratch at her pride. She had opted out of the trip as a strong and independent woman and going back on that decision seemed weak.

Betty was different, and this had appealed to Sara for a time. But the fact that Betty was so consistently negative, that she always tore things down: people, ideas, concepts, other types of music, this became tedious to Sara. Betty's most recent invitation for Sara to come over to her apartment and hang out, meaning drink a glass or two of wine and climb into bed, was declined.

"I kind of have some stuff I have to do for my father," said Sara into the telephone.

She was sitting at the desk in her room, a book of free verse poetry on her lap.

"What kind of stuff?" asked Betty.

"Just errands. You know, pick a bunch of stuff up for him. Now that Pei Ling is pretty much gone all the time, I have to do some of the stuff she used to do."

There was staticky silence as each woman waited for the other to speak.

"Give me a call if you want to hang out some time," said Betty.

Her voice was terse, more so than usual. The dial tone reached Sara's hearing before she could offer up a response of any kind.

Dobro and Sara met Pei Ling for lunch two days before she was scheduled to fly to China for a month-long visit. Once fully entrenched in her residency, she knew these visits home would become more difficult to arrange. There was the work schedule to consider, but of no doubt greater importance was the fact that once she fully exited the Dobro Temple sphere of influence, she would be paying her own way. Trips home, including the one she was about to embark on, were all arranged for by Dobro's assistant Angelica and paid for by the *Dobro Temple Agency* credit card she kept in her desk drawer outside Dobro's office. Pei Ling never took these kindnesses for granted and always offered to pay for them herself. But Dobro was always casually dismissive.

"It's a plane ticket, Pei Ling. You're family."

Pei Ling had selected a deli in Santa Monica when Angelica had called to arrange lunch.

"He wants you to pick the place. The lunch is kind of in your honor. A thank you kind of thing. And also, for your success in med school."

Never nearing what anyone would describe as touchy-feely with their collective interactions, Dobro and Sara both hugged Pei Ling when they joined her at the table she had taken. Sara's embrace was full on. She had not realized until this moment how important a person Pei Ling had been in her life.

"I'm going to miss you so much," she said as Pei Ling stood somewhat uncomfortably in her arms.

"Me, too," said Dobro as he replaced Sara in hugging Pei Ling.

His embrace did not extend below the chest and was much quicker. In all of these years, it was the first time the two of them had experienced anything more intimate than a handshake.

They all ordered iced tea. Sara had a turkey sandwich; Dobro selected a fresh salad piled high with sliced meat and hard-boiled eggs; Pei Ling went with her usual...matzo ball soup with a grilled cheese sandwich. Dobro loved many things about this woman, the eclectic nature of the foods she enjoyed among them.

"I got you something, Pei Ling," said Sara.

She slid a small box across the table. Pei Ling kept her hands on her lap, unsure of whether or not to accept it.

"Take it, Pei Ling," said Sara. "God, we may never see each other again. It's something to remember me by."

"But I didn't get you anything," said Pei Ling.

"All the stuff you've done for me. All the crap I put you through all these years. Believe me, Pei Ling, you've given me more than I can ever tell you."

Pei Ling picked up the box and inspected it thoroughly before removing the dark green wrapping paper.

"They're jade," said Sara as Pei Ling admired the earrings. "I thought that was kind of cool. You know because you're from China and all of that."

"They're beautiful, Sara. Thank you so much. I'll wear them often and I will think of you each time I do."

"I have a little something for you, too," said Dobro. He was smiling. Sara had not told him that she was getting a gift for Pei Ling, and the thoughtfulness on display at this moment pleased him greatly. Together, the two of them, he and this woman from China, had raised a caring and kind person. He owed Pei Ling a tremendous debt of gratitude, and this awareness washed over him as he sat sipping his tea. Although Pei Ling's presence in the day-to-day family dynamic had dissipated to almost nothing, the thought of her permanent absence was disquieting. He shared in her excitement; in the pride she took at becoming a doctor. But he would miss her greatly, and this was hitting him full-on for the first time.

"Your car," he said as he slid an envelope across the table. "Here's the title. You'll just have to get the paperwork changed at the DMV. And get some cheap insurance. If you call Angelica, she can help you with that."

Since he had first purchased a car for Pei Ling's use in helping run errands and in driving Sara from here to there, he had upgraded every four years. The current model, a small four-door German sedan, was only a year old.

"I can't accept this, Mr. Temple."

"Sure, you can," said Dobro just as the waiter arrived with sandwiches and Pei Ling's soup. "Just call Angelica about the insurance. She'll get you all set up."

The remainder of the lunch was quiet, as if not one of them was willing to disturb the moment. The air surrounding them was heavy with unspoken emotion; no one seemed willing to take too deep a breath for fear that in exhaling, strong feelings might be released.

In the lot as they said good-byes, all three of them returned to a slightly more formal demeanor. Dobro and Pei Ling again hugged in an almost perfunctory manner. Sara allowed Pei Ling to take her hands as the two women stood eye-to-eye, face-to-face. The reality of the fact that the fourteen plus years they had spent together was ending washed down on them like sunshine. Sara's entire life; almost half of Pei Ling's.

"Take care of yourself," said Pei Ling. "Call me. Call me. Promise?"

"I do," said Sara. "And you take care of yourself, too, Pei Ling."

Sara moved closer and brushed her cheek on Pei Ling's face.

"And when you get a boyfriend," whispered the young woman, "make sure you practice safe sex, Pei Ling."

Sara's smile was impish and almost boy-like. Pei Ling had seen it for years and loved the insouciance it projected. She would miss it along with everything else.

"How come you never go on dates?"

"How do you know that I don't go on dates? I could be a dating machine and you just don't know it."

Sara and her father sat at the conference table at one end of his rather spacious office. She had phoned and asked if he wanted her to surprise him with Chinese for lunch. They sat at the round table and ate expertly out of their containers with chopsticks. Among so many other things, this was a tiny piece of Pei Ling's legacy; Sara was proficient by the age of three.

"No, really. I mean, you hang with all these stars, all the shiny people. Aren't you ever tempted to date any of them? Aren't you ever enticed?"

Dobro chewed and swallowed.

"This is really good," he said. "And I'll tell you, those two words, tempted and enticed, are not words I would associate with wanting to date someone. In my opinion, they're the wrong words, the wrong motivation."

"What are the right words?" asked Sara.

Dobro looked out the window. The tops of palm trees from the street below were visible. He loved this office, the exposed brick, the framed faces of several of his clients and friends. Todd Rundgren, Delilah Duncan, William Hurt.

"Fascination. Intrigue. Maybe personal growth. Those are good motivations to date someone."

"So, those words never popped into your mind when you met someone? Nobody ever fascinated you or intrigued you?"

"You know, Sara, this job can be pretty all-consuming. And for a long time, I wanted to be able to give you a hundred present of my energy when I wasn't working. I did go out on a few dates when you were little, and Pei Ling was around to stay with you. I bet you didn't know that did you?"

"I did not," said Sara. "When I was a little girl, I used to think that you and Pei Ling would get married. I think I kind of secretly hoped for it. I even asked her one time if she was going to marry you."

This made Dobro smile.

"What'd she say?" he asked.

"She just did that thing that she always did where she blew out this enormous breath and rolled her eyes."

Dobro's smile had not left his face.

"I miss Pei Ling," he said. "She was a godsend for us. Both of us."

"I miss her, too. I called her last week and we talked for about half an hour. Get this…she actually has a boyfriend. Some guy from Poland who's working as a janitor at the hospital. He was an engineer or something back in Poland, and he's working there while he gets certified to work here. Isn't that cool? She's crazy busy, but you know her, she loves the shit out of it."

Dobro looked down at his container of food.

"That's an expression I don't think I've heard coming from you," he said without looking up.

"Sorry," said Sara. "I must be hanging out with a bad crowd or something."

Sara Temple's collection of friends was more varied than that of most young women her age, but this was to be expected. As she grew into adulthood and became more noticeably independent, she was exposed to many of her father's clients. After Betty Bonzo, she was relatively certain that her taste ran more towards men than women, but she remained open-minded and adventurous. This was Southern California after all.

Her father took her to all the glitzy events. She met actors at the Oscars and Emmy's, musicians from all genres at the Grammy's. There were dinners and parties and performances that her schoolmates would have died to be able to attend. Sara did not take all this for granted. For all the glamor surrounding her, she did her best to remain a down-to-earth woman.

David Iraq was a guitar player her father had represented for just over a year when she met him. His hair was long and was stringy from not being washed. He wore baggy clothing and a beard of four or five days' growth.

"I've heard your band," she said after they had been introduced at a fund-raising art show. Iraq was leaning against one of two bars in the large room. Dobro had approached him, Sara in tow, to say hello. When introduced to his agent's daughter, his demeanor did not change. He looked tired of the taste of the air he was breathing. He emanated the affectation of *young man suffering through the tediousness of life.* He did his best to endure. He was sure that those around him could see and feel this.

"Did you like it?"

"I liked it a lot," said Sara.

Her father had excused himself and had moved to another circle of conversation.

"You're a great guitar player, and I really liked the lyrics in your songs."

"I work at it," said Iraq. "A lot of people think that musicians, *good* musicians, just pick up an instrument and play. But I work my ass off. I'm like some guy writing a great book or something. I really am."

There was silence as Sara searched for something to say. She had just turned seventeen and was by no means shy or incapable of carrying on meaningful discussion. But this man seemed daunting to her in his distance, in his sullenness. She wanted desperately to appear as someone other than a sparkly-eyed high school student.

"Do you know Betty Bonzo?" she asked.

David Iraq looked at her as if he just that moment noticed her standing there.

"Yeah. I know her. You?"

"I kind of dated her a while ago."

As soon as the words were out of her mouth, she wanted them back. This was a child's attempt to appear cool, and she knew that Iraq would see it as such.

"What do you think of her music? Of her bands' music?" he said.

"What I just told you about me dating her, can that stay between us? And I don't really care for her music. It's too loud and I get tired of the negativity."

"So, what was she like to date?" he asked.

Sara felt herself blushing. Again, she scoured her brain for the right words to use.

"She's…forceful. You know what I mean? I mean, she doesn't do anything just-a-little-bit. She goes all in. She's intense."

David Iraq looked at her once more. His glance left her face and moved to her toes and then back.

"You know what we should do?" he said.

"What's that," said Sara.

"We should get together sometime and talk music. I'm really curious to hear more about Betty."

Sara knew what her response to this should have been. It was clear and was not clouded with ambiguity. It was a line in a play, not to be deviated from. It was a swift declination of this offer followed by a quick turn to where her father was now standing.

"That sounds like fun," she heard herself saying with a voice she did not recognize. "But we would probably have to keep it to ourselves."

"Give me your number," said David Iraq.

For all of his railing against the mainstream and the trappings of materialism, David lived in a very nice home in Hollywood Hills. It was small, but the floors were made of brilliantly blue and orange ceramic tiles. The furnishings were modern, oak and iron predominating; large windows let in sufficient natural light, enough to please a painter.

Sara parked in the driveway and checked her appearance in the rear view mirror. She smiled to check her teeth; she exhaled loudly in an effort to slow her heart rate. As she walked to the door of David Iraq's house, she spit the piece of cinnamon-flavored gum she had been chewing into a shrub.

Sara was as adventurous as the next young woman, but she had always been able to maintain a sense of equilibrium when it came to making decisions. She was not frightened or daunted by the situation she was striding towards. But one of those voices deep, deep inside her head was talking to her. It was not screaming. It was simply telling her, in a calm and instructive manner, to keep her bearings.

"Hey, you found me," said David as he greeted her at the door.

The weather was perfect, warm with little to no humidity. He pushed open the screen door and stepped back to make room for Sara to enter. Windows throughout the living room were open and a gentle breeze cooled the house. He wore a pair of baggy shorts and an ages-old white dress shirt unbuttoned. His feet were bare.

She inspected him as surreptitiously as possible, a peak here, a furtive glance there. Tall, thin, not much chest hair, brown eyes, hair to his shoulders.

"Good directions," she said as she stepped onto the tile floor. "Wow. What a beautiful home you have here. It's really not what I expected."

"How so? What did you expect?"

She dropped her bag, a green cloth catch-all with a shoulder strap, in a chair as she entered.

"I don't know. I was thinking maybe a loft or an abandoned warehouse or something. No furniture. Just a table and a chair. Maybe some recording equipment. But this is really nice, David. It's very homey."

"Just don't tell anybody," he said. "I have an image to uphold, you know?"

They sat in the living room, David on the sofa, Sara in an easy chair. A coffee table with a candle at each end separated them.

"Want something to drink?" he asked. "I don't have much of a selection. I have some bottled water and a few beers. Want a beer, Sara?"

"Sure," she said. "Can I come see your kitchen?"

He stood and waved her in front of him. As she stepped past him, she sensed just a hint of shampoo. And he had shaved.

"I'm surprised again," she said. "No dishes in the sink. Neat as a pin in here."

He smiled as he took two bottles of beer from the refrigerator.

"Well, I work hard at keeping my place nice," he said. "And I write a check a couple times a week to the lady who comes in and cleans for me. Full disclosure. She just left about an hour ago."

They sat in the airy and bright living room and sipped their beers. It was quiet, the stillness only broken by their words and the barking of a dog somewhere down the lane.

"Okay, I have to ask," said Sara, "why did you invite me to visit you? Surely, you have to have far more interesting women circling your world than me."

He sipped his beer and placed the bottle on the table at his knees.

"You're real," he said. "You probably know this from hanging out with your father, with the people he represents and all of that. But it's refreshing to meet someone who isn't all committed to acting a certain way…in a way that they think they're supposed to be acting. You don't have any of that. I liked who you were at the core the minute I met you."

"I get it," she said. "You're different. Not that I've met a ton of people in the world of entertainment or anything like that. But the few I *have* met, you're different. In a good way. I can tell from sitting here for ten minutes with you, that you're genuine."

"What was Betty like?" he asked.

"What is your fascination with Betty Bonzo? Do you have a crush on her or something?"

He laughed.

"God no. I just wonder how it works that people with zero fucking talent can make it big. I mean, you've heard their albums, right?"

Sara nodded.

"Yeah. Not a fan. Betty's alright. But I think the loudness, the constant tearing down of people and stuff, I think it's a sign of insecurity. She seems like a lonely little girl to me."

"I shouldn't ask this…I know I shouldn't ask this…"

"Yes," said Sara. "We did. And that's all I'm going to say about that. Be a gentleman, David. I'm sure that's what your parents raised you to be."

The remainder of the afternoon flowed smoothly by, the breeze through the window just enough, but not too much. They looked at photo albums, David played the guitar, he made nachos as they each drank a second beer. As the afternoon sky began to shade into a darker blue, Sara rose to leave.

"I have to be going," she said. "Man, this has been a lot of fun. Thank you so much for inviting me."

He stood and walked her to the door.

"Serious question," he said. "Are you one hundred percent certain that you're good to drive?"

"I am. I didn't even finish my second beer. I only drank half of it."

"Two more questions, and then I'll let you go."

"Shoot," she said.

"One, would you like to come back some afternoon and hang out with me?"

"That sounds really nice," she said. "What's the second question?"

"Does your father know you're here?"

This struck Sara as important. The question contained a hint of implication that this was wrong, that this had been wrong, that it should be hidden and not discussed with anyone else. But she was a strong and independent woman just then, and the beer she had enjoyed with this charismatic and caring musician was reminding her of her own sense of self.

"I think what I decide to do with you is my business and not anyone else's," she said.

He walked her to her car and opened the door for her.

"Be careful driving," he said.

That he had not kissed her or even shook her hand did not bother her as she drove towards Topanga Canyon. This was serious, grown-up stuff. And she liked it greatly.

The third time Sara visited David Iraq at his home in the Hollywood Hills, a Friday, he gave her a guitar. It was a delicately aged Alvarez, and it played easily with rich tones, particularly at the higher range. He showed her how to play two chords and gave her a book of beginner exercises. He then led her into his bedroom, slowly removed her jeans and top and kissed her. Betty Bonzo was a passionate kisser, she recalled; David was passionate but in a gentler and more cautious way. She removed her underwear and slid into the covers on his bed with the delicateness of a ballerina.

"My God, you have a beautiful body," he said as he ran his hand across her breasts and down to her tight and flat stomach.

"It's all the swimming," she said with a voice slightly cracked.

He kissed her once more and she could feel her heart beating. This was not fumbling through the episode with a high school boy or trying your best to be a good sport with a woman you were not truly attracted to. This was pure and this was elemental. Sara swam in the feelings of the moment. She made great effort at cataloguing the details for her memory's sake. The way his hands felt on her; the taste of his tongue; a moment of delay as he unwrapped a condom and placed it on his penis; the sensation of being fully yet gently entered. At the end, when she felt a wave wash over her, she could think of nothing but her own pleasure.

He made cups of strong coffee and brought them back to bed. They sat with their backs to the headboard and sipped their drinks.

"That was pretty wonderful," said Sara.

"Agreed," he said. "I haven't done that in a long time."

"You're a big time musician. That statement cannot be true."

"Like I said the first time you came here, I find most of the people I meet to be less than interesting. They're not real. They don't have any substance."

She sipped her drink, careful not to burn her mouth or spill any on the thick quilt that covered her legs up to her waist.

"So, I have substance?"

He thought for several seconds. The windows were open, and the afternoon breeze carried a hint of jasmine. It was as close to a perfect moment as he could imagine.

"Now that you have a guitar, you bet your ass you have substance."

Later in the afternoon he made sandwiches and brewed more coffee. They sat at the table in his kitchen. He asked about her plans after high school, she asked what it was like to perform in front of so many people. The conversation was comfortable. They each listened more than they spoke.

When David had loaded her guitar into the back seat of her car, and after he had kissed her one last time through the open window as she sat behind the steering wheel, she drove away. He wondered how in hell a girl, a woman that young, could have so much assuredness and poise. He also reveled in her scent on his fingertips as he brought his hand to his face.

"Where'd you get the guitar?"

She had been surprised to see her father's car in the drive when she got home. It was a Friday night, not yet six, and he rarely arrived home before seven.

She thought of simply leaving the guitar in her back seat until the next day when she could quietly bring it to her room, but David had warned her against this. Heat or cold were bad for the bracing of the instrument; the neck could warp. And Sara also knew that the discussion that loomed on the immediate horizon, that telling her father about David Iraq, was an eventuality. She suspected that she could have held on to the secret for a while but didn't really want to.

"It's from that guy I met at that party with you, David Iraq. He gave it to me."

Dobro had been reading a magazine, his glasses perched on the bridge of his nose. He sat in an easy chair, his back to the windows looking out over the canyon, his feet resting on a cushioned footstool. He sat up, feet on the ground and removed his glasses.

"My David Iraq?" he said. "My client David Iraq?"

"You know how you always said I could share anything with you?" said Sara, "how I could tell you anything? Well, David and I have been kind of seeing each other a little bit. And I don't want to sneak around and mislead you on any of this. He gave me the guitar."

"Sara, the man is ten, eleven years older than you. What are you doing?"

"Dad, I'm going to be eighteen in a few months. I'm going to be going off to college or wherever in less than a year. You have to have a little faith in my ability to make good decisions. He's a very nice guy. A very nice man. He's interesting and fun to hang out with. Do you have to make a big deal about his age?"

Dobro Temple was not a knee jerk reaction kind of guy. He processed before he proceeded. He stood and moved to where Sara was standing, guitar case still in hand.

Dobro took the case from her and gently set it on the floor. He placed one hand on each of her shoulders and looked directly into her blue eyes. He spoke softly.

"I have enormous faith in you," he said. "I really do. But I also know that not every decision you make, not every decision any of us make, is the right one. I make mistakes all the time, and I own those. And what I want you to understand right now is that this is a mistake you're making. It doesn't feel like it, but you have to believe me. It is. This is where you need to have faith in me. In the fact that I've seen more things in life, that I recognize situations that aren't right. And this is one of them."

"Are you saying all of this because it's an age thing, or because he's your client?" she asked without looking away from him.

He removed his hands from her shoulders.

"A little of one; a lot of the other. Listen, Sara, I'm not going to demand anything from you. I know more about these types of things, this type of thing, than you do, and I hope you'll give this enough thought to arrive at the same conclusion…the same sense of what you should and should not do. I don't want you hurt and I don't want you used, and I know you think David is all wonderful and incapable of doing anything like that, but I know the lay of the land better than you. I know deep, deep down that the best thing for you to do is to be dating boys, men, closer to your age."

She was angry and he knew this. The warmth that seemed always to be in the blueness of her eyes had turned to ice.

"I'm going to think about all of this," she said. "But I'm not making any promises."

"That's all I can ask," said Dobro. "Did you have dinner?"

"We ate at David's," she said with a slightly contemptuous tone.

She picked up her guitar and stepped toward her room.

"And you need to know, Dad," she said without turning back to him, "that there's a really good chance that we're in love with each other."

Dobro Temple arrived at his office at seven the next morning. He checked on Sara before leaving. She slept soundly as he peaked in through the slightly cracked door.

He left a note on the kitchen counter telling her that he would be back by noon, although he anticipated being home much sooner.

Waiting in his office were two men, both casually dressed. Khaki shorts and golf shirts seemed to be the uniform of the day.

"Thank you both for coming in today. Sorry if this interrupted plans, but we'll be out of here in an hour or so."

Seated at the round conference table were the two people Dobro Temple trusted most in life. They may in fact have been the only people to have earned this distinction, that of being trusted unconditionally.

The shorter and heavier-set of the two was William Carlson. An attorney who had grown up in the San Fernando Valley, been educated at Southern Cal and then the Pepperdine Law School, he had risen to a position of prominence by being thorough. This was Southern California. Glitz and splash abounded. But people like William Carlson, "Bilbo" to those close to him, were possessed of neither of these qualities. He got stuff done. On time and as promised, he delivered the goods. Dobro was not his only client, but he had been one of the first. The bond that existed between these two "handlers of the stars" was solid as a tree trunk. They had been through the battles of celebrity warfare and were, for the most part, unscarred.

The other man carried a more serious demeanor about him. Paul Danko had completed two tours of duty in Vietnam. He talked little about his time spent in Southeast Asia, but on the rare occasion of consuming one-too many cocktails at a Dobro event, he would share miniscule slivers of his experiences with his boss.

"The choppers used to drop us on hills, half-way down. It was difficult for the enemy to get to us from either above or below, at least for a matter of minutes. We'd be out there for days. We would just tear ass around the place looking for stuff to destroy. Anything that even hinted of military value, and a lot of stuff that didn't. Bridges made from ropes and logs, anything close to resembling a structure that could house munitions, tunnels and caves, anyone that seemed to have a nefarious look to them. That last part was especially troubling to a lot of men. A lot of the guys I served with carried that home with them and were never able to come to grips with it."

Dobro always listened attentively on the rare occasion that Paul Danko spoke of such things. Paul interested him greatly. He was many things Dobro was not, but the two men had meaningful things in common. Both were serious and both were calculating; to a man, they were rarely surprised by any turn of event.

Danko had joined a security firm immediately upon being discharged from the Marine Corps, had learned the business from bottom to top, and had then forged out on his own. He was expert at convincing potential clients that his company was the best possible solution to their concerns, and he always followed through. If he committed to something, his clients could rest assured that it would be done. This steadfastness and attention to the idiosyncratic needs of his rather specialized clientele made him successful and much sought after. That Dobro was the client he placed on top of his list was a result of their mutual trust in each other, and from the fact that neither man had ever been untruthful with the other.

Paul Danko was a tall man with broad shoulders. His blond hair was cut short, and he was always clean shaven. He wore high-end clothing and had a disarming smile. Almost every woman he met was intrigued by him and many conversations hinted at a desire to get to know him better. The men he encountered did not share this outlook. They most certainly did not want Danko to know them better than he already did.

Dobro joined the men at the table. He took a deep breath and folded his hands together as if about to pray.

"I need a couple things done. Today, if possible. This morning would be even better."

"What can I do?" asked Bilbo.

"I need a letter crafted ending my relationship with someone."

"Who's the someone," asked the attorney. "By the way, coffee for anyone. Dobro, I took the liberty of making a pot."

"Yeah," said Dobro.

He continued to speak as he rose and walked across the office to the coffee pot.

"David Iraq," he said, his back to the conference table. "I need my relationship with him ended immediately."

The men at the table were silent until he had returned and was again seated with them.

"Can we know why?" asked Paul Danko. "This is a bit out of the ordinary for you, Dobro."

"He seduced my daughter. All the shit I've for done for this man, all the money I've made for him, and he does this."

"Jesus Christ," said Bilbo Carlson, "how old is Sara now?"

"She's seventeen and a few months. And she's just been overwhelmed by his whole deal. The guy oozes charm, let's be honest. He bought her a fucking guitar for Christ sakes."

The three men digested what had just been spit on the table.

"I can draw up the letter in ten minutes," said Bilbo. "This is clearly within your rights, even if it wasn't your daughter. We have a moral turpitude clause in the standard contract. The fact that Sara is under eighteen…well, you know."

"Good. You can sit at Angelica's desk. There's a set of keys to the files. It's in her top drawer, probably under an envelope or something. The file cabinets on the wall opposite her desk have all the client information. They're very up-to-date. Let me know if you can't find his file. I truly appreciate this, Bilbo."

When the attorney had positioned himself at the desk in the outer office, Paul Danko spoke in a lower voice to Dobro.

"And you would like me to deliver the letter," he said.

The two men had coordinated efforts many times on activities that often bordered the boundaries of legality. Occasionally, the boundary was crossed, but only when absolutely necessary. The broken fingers on the right hand of the man who supplied one of Dobro's clients with heroin; the listening devices placed on the phones of a client's husband in the midst of a messy divorce and custody battle; the not-too-terribly-subtle threat of a beating if money owed another of Dobro's clients was not forthcoming. Neither man enjoyed these episodes. But neither of them shied away from these decisions when this work was necessary.

Dobro nodded.

"I don't want him hurt or threatened, although that's tempting. The guy's fucked half the city. He's a player and he's just using my daughter."

"Okay," said Paul, icy stare not leaving Dobro's eyes.

"I would like him told that it might be in his best interest to never contact Sara again. Maybe you mention that what he's been doing, what he's probably been doing, as much as I hate thinking about it, is statutory rape. She's a minor, and that little prick is at least ten years older than she is. Maybe you mention that you have some evidence of that, and that you'd really prefer not to talk to your friends at the LAPD. Just get him out of Sara's life, Paul. Please."

Paul Danko had never married. He was well known as a lady's man. Handsome, rugged, well off financially. To his knowledge, he had never fathered a child. He had been with Dobro throughout Sara's life, and the girl was as close to a substitute, surrogate daughter as anyone could have possibly been.

"I'll shake his hand before I leave," said Danko. "No follow up visit will be necessary."

Sara's car was gone when Dobro returned to the house in Topanga. He peaked into her room to make sure she was not somehow home. It appeared as it always did; clothes in the laundry hamper, shoes and sandals lined up along the wall. The larger of her two windows was opened, but only slightly.

Dobro went to the kitchen and fetched a bottle of beer from the refrigerator. Not a big drinker, especially at eleven in the morning, it simply felt like the thing to do as he waited for his daughter to return. He knew that there would be fireworks, but that this was necessary.

He gave some thought to calling Pei Ling, but quickly dismissed this idea. These two women who were so predominant in his life had developed their own bond based on trust and silence. As much as he wanted Pei Ling's insights and support, he was reluctant to impose upon her relationship with Sara. Only in an emergency, he thought to himself.

Dobro sat on the deck with a book he had a hard time reading. His focus simply was not there as he waited for Sara to come home.

She returned a little after three, pulling into the driveway a little faster than usual. Dobro watched her exit the vehicle and shut her car door with an extra flourish. He watched her climb the stairs to the deck and waited without moving for her to make eye contact with him.

She appeared calm, but he knew from the few episodes of disagreement they had lived through, that this was not unusual. Pei Ling was the face of stoicism, and he was a master of calculation. It was no wonder to him that his daughter had grown up to be thinker; hair-trigger reactions were not in her repertoire.

She sat in a lounge chair a few feet from him. His one bottle of beer rested empty on the table beside him.

"Why couldn't you have simply talked to me?" she asked. "If me seeing David was such a big deal, why couldn't we just have talked it out?"

He paused before answering.

"A couple things, Sara. I don't know to what end we could have had a discussion like that. I was not, I *am not*, going to allow my daughter who's not even eighteen yet, have an affair with someone like David Iraq. I know things you don't, and that was just going to end up in you and I disagreeing. I think a conversation like that would have been a waste of time. Neither of us had any prayer of changing each other's mind on this."

"What's the second thing, before I even think about responding to that?" she asked.

"The second thing is that what happened today, that I don't represent him any longer, that would have happened if I'd learned that he was having a relationship with *anyone* your age. I don't fool around with this stuff, and you know that. He's not the first client I dumped because of stuff like this. Had he been fooling around with anyone else's daughter, the outcome of today would have been the same. Except you wouldn't be sitting there pissed at me."

"You didn't trust me," she said. "You will never know how much that hurt me."

"The way you were last night, the way you acted about the whole thing...I mean, you almost rubbed my nose in it, Sara. We've talked about this. Who we are, who we become, this is all based on relationships we experience along the way. People touch us in good and damaging ways, and I saw this as a potentially very damaging way. I just can't let it happen."

"Is it that we were having sex?" she asked.

This question would cut her father, and she knew it.

"No," he said. "Maybe a little. I'm not naïve. I'm not stupid. You're almost eighteen. I was young once, too. It wasn't that so much as I take very seriously my role to protect you from harm and to do my best to keep you on a good path. This was not a good path."

"Well, keeper-of-the-good-path, you don't need to worry anymore. Mr. Danko visited David and scared the shit out of him. David wouldn't even let me in when I went over there. We talked through a window, like I was visiting someone in prison."

"I hope you can see that what happened was with your best interest in mind," he said. "I know you're angry, but please try to understand that, okay?"

Sara rose and stepped towards the sliding door that led into the house.

"I don't hate you. You need to know that. And I know that in some fucked up way, you feel what you did today was right. But it wasn't. And you need to know that, too."

She entered the house and went into her room, closing the door behind her. Dobro sat beside the pool for a few minutes longer. He gave some thought to dinner, wondering if Sara would eat. There was the risk that she would carry this anger with her for a long time. He knew that this day might well alter the dynamic between the two of them for years. But the events of this day had not been negotiable. He was committed unconditionally to his role as this woman's father, and the fallout from his actions had never been a consideration.

Of interest to Dobro as he stood and moved toward the house was the fact that this was the first time he had heard his daughter use the word *fuck.*

It took Sara two months before she could sit comfortably with her father. It was not from any act of forgiveness that she came to this place. Time can heal most wounds. That, and the fact that David Iraq was seen on the covers of grocery store tabloids with a new woman just about every week helped her move past the argument with her father. The women captured by paparazzi were all hanging on David's arm, they were all attractive and very young. Sara was sure they all spoke to his creative genius when asked, and she wondered how many of them he had bought guitars.

She was thinker, a contemplator. Growing up with Pei Ling and her father would not have allowed her to become anything but this. As Sara met more and more of her father's clients, she also began to see him through their eyes. He was a source of strength for many of them, a savior for others.

"Your daddy stretched the limits of his comfort zone when he took me on."

This was from Billy Joe Rundle, a recovering abuser of drugs and alcohol, whose career in country music had been restored to health by Dobro. Sara had accompanied her father to another of his client receptions, and she had stayed to chat with Rundle after having been introduced to him.

"I had just got out of jail...I was in San Quentin for forty-five months for aggravated assault...I shot a guy who owed me money on a drug deal that went bad...thank God he didn't die...and your daddy agreed to meet with me. A guy I knew through the record company, my old company, had worked with your daddy years before, and he suggested I ask if he'd take me on. Told me he was a very honest man. Can you imagine? As straight an arrow as your daddy is, that he would agree to give someone like me a second chance?"

Sara took him in. A large man with long black hair and a heavy beard. His eyes were somewhere on the scale between wet tree bark and onyx. His hands were covered with prison tattoos: poorly-drawn Yin and Yang, a heart, several crucifixes. He wore black jeans and a leather jacket over a white collared shirt.

"I'm sorry I haven't heard any of your music," said Sara. "I'll ask my dad to get me a CD. That's quite a journey you've been on, and I bet it comes through in the songs you do."

"It does. I found Jesus in prison…doesn't everybody? Either Jesus or Allah? And my music reflects that. At least I think it does. I'm not all holy roller kind of shit, don't get me wrong. But I tend to put a positive spin on things now. In the old days, everything was pretty dark all around me. What do you do, Sara? Enough about my old story."

He had a gravelly voice from thousands of cigarettes and countless shots of cheap whiskey, but Sara found it comforting. Despite his appearance, outlaw country music star, she found herself trusting him. Yet again, her father's intuition was spot on. As much as she didn't want to admit it, evidence of Dobro Temple's prescience filled the room.

"I'm in my last year of high school, and then I'll probably go to college. My dad and I are visiting a place next week in fact."

"Pretty, smart girl like you, with a strong father standing behind her…you'll go far I bet. But can I tell you one thing? Can I give you one little piece of advice even though we only just met each other?"

Rundle was looking down and directly into her eyes. He was smiling knowingly; a child knowing what was in the gift box he was about to open.

"Sure," she said. "I'll take all the advice I can get."

Rundle placed his hand on her shoulder.

"Don't forget about God," he said. "Don't forget to let Him lead the way. Make all the decisions you need to make, but don't forget to ask His opinion before you make 'em."

She nodded with exaggerated solemnity.

"Thank you, Mr. Rundle. That's probably really good advice, and I'll do that."

"The next time you see me, you're going to have to call me Billy Joe, okay, Sara?"

"Yes, sir," she said.

She asked her father about Rundle on the way home.

"Quite a character," he said as he drove the winding road up into the canyon. "Did he tell you his life story?"

"Yeah, but he's not scary at all. A guy who's done all the stuff he's done, that guy should be scary a little, right? But he's not. I found him to be very trustworthy."

Dobro gave that some thought before responding.

"There's nothing wrong with trusting people, Sara. It's a good character trait. But I always make sure I know all the ins and outs about someone before I extend that trust too far. You know? The more I get to know them, the more I feel I can trust them."

"That sounds a little calculating, dad. Don't you ever meet someone, and you just know they're worthy of your trust?"

"I have met people like that…that I just took in all the way immediately. And they turned out to be the only people I've ever been scorched by. Maybe you can read people better than I can, but I always make people earn my trust. It's safer, believe me."

When Betty Bonzo called, Sara was on her way out the door to visit Barrow College in Northern California with her father. It was a small school with an enrollment of just over a thousand located in the town from which it took its name. Barrow offered a diverse catalogue of fields from which students could earn undergraduate degrees. Admission standards were higher than many of the other schools Sara and her father were considering, but this presented no problem; Sara had been an excellent student throughout her life. With Pei Ling and her father as role models, she truly could not have been anything but this.

"Wow, I didn't expect to be hearing from you. How are you?" said Sara.

She was sitting on her bed, a bag of clothes packed for the trip beside her. She was wearing the sandals Betty had given her.

"I'm good. I'm doing well. I just got this notion of calling you. I was thinking of you the other day. I can't even remember what triggered it. Anyway, I just thought I'd call and say hello. What are you up to? Messing around with all those high school boys still?"

Sara frowned, but with a slight smile.

"Not so much. I'm actually headed to the airport right now. My dad and I are visiting a school up north. I'm kind of narrowing my choices down. But this one, it's Barrow College, it sounds really nice. How's the music biz?"

"We're doing alright. I never got a chance to talk much about it, you know, before you dumped me and everything…"

"I did not dump you, Betty," said Sara in full grin. "I can't even remember what happened. I was probably just busy when you called that time."

"I'm fucking with you, girl. It's all good. But I never got a chance to bitch about life in a band. It's what I do best… bitch about the hands that feed me."

This made Sara smile again. As negative and gloomy as Betty seemed always to be, there was often a hint of sarcasm in her words; she never spared herself when in attack mode.

"Listen, I have a flight to catch, but I'll call you in a couple days when I'm back. Are you still in LA? Still at the same place?"

"No. I caved to the establishment and bought a house in the valley. It's not much, but it's way better than that shit hole I used to live in. Remember the green water in the pool?"

"I do," said Sara.

Perhaps it was the moment, the flight waiting to take her to potentially the newest installment of her growth into adulthood, the fact that her relationship with her father had returned to normal after the David Iraq affair, the awareness that very soon she would be leaving the house in Topanga and living on her own. She was not sure what drove the emotion. It was like hearing a random song on the radio while driving somewhere that, for no reason imaginable, filled her with happiness. Sara couldn't explain the comfortable feeling that washed over her just then. But she loved it.

"Okay," said Betty. "Call me when you get back. We're starting a mini-tour in a week. Just like eight shows. It would be a blast if you'd come along. You know, live the rock and roll life for ten days."

"I'll think about it, and I'll for sure give you a call when I'm back. It's good to hear from you, Betty."

"Ciao, baby," said Betty before hanging up.

The trip north was enjoyable. Angelica had procured seats in first class and had made certain a higher end rental car was waiting for them at the San Francisco airport. The drive to the town of Barrow was slightly over an hour, and the scenery as Dobro drove inland and away from the ocean was spectacular.

"This is a haul up here," said Dobro. "You sure you want to be this far away?"

"Well, you figure a flight and a couple hours in the car, I'm home in four hours or so," she said. "Wow, this is pretty, isn't it?"

"It is," said her father. "Is your friend Derry still planning on going here?"

Derry was a girl Sara had gone through twelve years of school with. Although they were never what either of them would call best friends, they shared a genuine sense of comfort in each other's company. Each represented a familiarity of place to the other. If both women decided on Barrow, it was their plan to share a dorm room.

"Yup. She's already done pre-registration stuff."

"Well, that's comforting. At least you'll have someone from home with you if you decide to come up here."

Sara was ever-so-slightly detached for the remainder of the car ride and through the tour of campus. The antiquated beauty of the buildings, the tree-covered hills in every direction, the cafes, pubs and shops that catered to a college-aged clientele, all were exactly what she had hoped for. But she couldn't get Betty Bonzo out of her head. She had an itch to see what being on tour was like, and she decided to talk to her father about it on the flight home.

He did not say no. Although the *let's-wait-and-see* ploy had never worked with Sara, there being no other parent with whom to check, in addition to her naturally-acquired tenacity, Sara's father went with it on this occasion. They had just taken off and settled into their seats for the short flight.

"I'm only saying that I want to make a phone call. I'd like the dates and places of the tour stops. This is just normal, concerned parent stuff, Sara. At first blush, I'm not terrifically opposed to it. Just give me a day."

"Fair enough," she said. "I just think it would be fun, and it would be a nice, little adventure before starting school. Think of it like summer camp, dad"

That afternoon, when they had returned to the house in Topanga and Sara was cloistered in her bedroom phoning friends about the decision she had made to attend Barrow, Dobro called Margo Malone.

"Aloha, Dobro. And to what do I owe this great honor, you calling me on a Saturday?"

"Aloha back, Margo. I hope I'm not bothering you. Is this a good time that I could ask you a couple things? Somewhat personal things?"

"Of course, it's a good time. Personal things? I'm intrigued."

Her voice was deep and hoarse, as if she'd smoked cigarettes packed with sawdust shavings for many years. It was man-like, and was Margo Malone's calling card, her distinguishing feature. That, and the articles of outer clothing made from animal pelts. Although there already existed a well-structured and serious movement to condemn this brand of cruelty to animals, she did not care. On more than one occasion she was splashed with fake blood by an animal lover attempting to make a point. If the point was made, it was not made on her. She was a frequent customer at *The House of Fur* on Rodeo Drive.

"Your client. Well, I assume she's still your client. Betty Bonzo."

"She's still with me. Her band is actually doing quite well. For the life of me, I can't understand anyone liking that music. But it's beginning to sell. What about her, Dobro?"

Dobro looked into the house. He could see that Sara's door was still closed.

"She's started a friendship with my daughter Sara. You remember Sara? You met her at one of my things."

"Beautiful girl, my friend. And so poised."

"So, Betty has invited Sara along on some tour they're getting ready to go on, and I just want some sort of sanity check on whether or not I should be concerned about letting her go. I mean, Sara's eighteen. She's an adult woman, as hard as that is for me to wrap my head around. I just would like some sort of feedback on how safe and controlled everything is. What's this Betty like?"

"Hold for one moment please, Dobro," said Margo. "I'll only be a second on this other call."

As he sat listening to silence, Dobro imagined Margo Malone sitting on a wide veranda sipping champagne and smoking elegantly from a four-inch cigarette holder. He pictured her hair encased in a turban. That she was sitting at her kitchen table wearing a bathrobe and a pair of furry slippers would have surprised him, but it would have made him smile.

"Sorry about that," she said as she clicked back to him. "Trying to get an appointment at a decent spa in this town is like trying to get a date with the Dalai Lama."

This made Dobro smile.

"So, where were we?" she said. "Oh yes. Betty. You want to know about Betty. Well, most simply put, Dobro, is that Betty is not really what her image portrays. She and the other screaming meanies in that band all come across as pretty bad-ass and wild. But I'll tell you honestly, my friend, that almost all of that is just image. It's just their brand. I've encouraged it. As I said, it's starting to sell."

"Drugs? Alcohol? Should I worry about any of that?" he asked.

"No. Not at all. And I would never steer you wrong on that. We've both seen way too many casualties from that lifestyle. I don't think Betty and her friends even use drugs. I'm not terribly sure they even drink. They're loud and can be absolutely obnoxious, but they all seem pretty benign, Dobro."

"Can I get the details on this tour from you, Margo? Just so I can have a sense of where they're going to be?"

"Of course, love. I'll have it shot over to you Monday morning, if that works."

"You're a delight, Margo. I'm a fortunate man to have you as a friend and a client."

"Tootles, love. Lunch soon."

Margo Malone placed the phone on the table and lit a new cigarette. As she smoked, she removed her very expensive wig of platinum-colored hair and dropped it next to the phone. She ran her hand across the top of her bald head as she inhaled the toxins she was sure would eventually kill her.

Sara didn't anticipate large stadiums or expansive concert halls. But neither did she expect county fairs. One stop on the tour, the second, in a small town in Nevada just miles from Las Vegas, she was surprised to find that the band was to play in a converted barn. The promoter, a tall and thin man dressed in jeans, a rhinestone shirt buttoned to the neck and the obligatory pair of cowboy boots, had bought the place from a failing rancher and built a stage opposite the large double doors. The rows of chairs, eighty or so, where the type rolled out for use in school cafeterias on parent and teacher nights. Small children performing an abridged Broadway musical. Dust from drying and decayed bales of straw still lingered in the air.

"I don't see how anybody makes any money," said Sara to Betty Bonzo.

Sara had helped the band set up their instruments and amplifying equipment. After a very brief and perfunctory sound check, she and Betty had returned to the tour bus. They sat at the table and were enjoying sandwiches and cold sodas. The driver of the bus and the other band members, three young women seemingly cut from the same cloth as

Betty, had taken the one car that accompanied the big bus and headed toward the neon splendor that is Las Vegas. They promised to return in plenty of time for the evening's concert and to bring snacks for afterward.

"It's not important. I know what you're thinking. This place is a dump and the guy promoting this gig must be doing something illegal to be able to make any money at all. But it's not our concern. We love to play for people. That's why we all got together in the first place, and it's why we put up with all the shit that comes along with having a band. We'd play on a street corner if that was all that was available to us. We do get paid, though. You learn that early in this biz. Get the money up front."

Sara chewed her sandwich with delicate bites. Betty drank her soda from the can and wiped her mouth with the back of her hand.

"I guess if it's what moves you," said Sara.

After a moment of reflection, of watching Betty take another giant bite from the sandwich she held in her left hand throughout the conversation, Sara wrapped what remained of her lunch in plastic paper and dropped it in a trash can resting beside the tiny table.

"I'm full," she said. "I think I'm going to take a little nap."

"Want some company?" asked Betty. "Not for any fooling around stuff. Just taking a nap kind of stuff. Little girls on a sleepover kind of stuff."

"Sure," said Sara not knowing why.

They crawled into the sleeping berth Sara had been using since joining the tour. It was crowded and warm. Sara was not sure she could sleep. She spent several minutes second guessing the decision to come on this trip. She knew that it was merely a phone call for her father to arrange for her speedy return home to Topanga. She could be swimming right now. She could be buying clothes she did not need in preparation for her trip to Barrow. But that would mean an acknowledgement of sorts, that her decision was not as forward thinking as it should have been, that she had acted rashly and had made a poor choice. It would mean owning up to these things, and she was not about to allow for that. When she woke forty minutes later, she and Betty were perspiring heavily and the stale, warm air of the bus was strongly scented with body odor.

The second from the last stop on the tour was at a Renaissance Fair in a Montana town proclaiming itself the trout capital of the world. The scenery was awe-inspiring, the townspeople slightly stand-offish. What a very loud, very brash band comprised of lesbians had to do with jousting, madrigals, falcon-hunting and blacksmiths Sara did not know. But the stage was solidly-built, and the crowd promised to be one of the larger assemblages the band would see. The weather was cool and clear, and there was a wide variety of offerings from the food trucks circled at one end of the open field.

The bus arrived on a Friday night. As the band was only one of several to be playing the following two days, it was not necessary to cart much of the sound equipment on stage. The bands would be sharing, and this made for a free night of playing cards and walking among the variety of tents and tables which would be selling goods and services the next day. Young people who would be dressed in full regalia in the morning were now sitting around fires in shorts and sweatshirts. There was some drinking, and Sara detected the whiff of pot being smoked. But the members of the troupe were subdued and pleasant. Bonfires seemed everywhere.

Sara and Betty walked through the makeshift village the next morning as exhibits were being set up. Men in leather pants and women in ground-length velvet dresses were busy placing merchandise of all kinds on the card tables the fair organizers had supplied each stand. Smoke from the food trucks at the far end of the open field wafted over the village. The morning was chilly but was certain to give way to a steamy afternoon.

"Want me to buy you a sword?" Betty asked Sara as they passed the silversmith booth.

"I'm not sure I would have much use for a sword, but thanks, anyway."

"You might need it to fight off all those college boys when you go to school in a couple weeks. Pretty girl like you. Those boys are going to lose their minds."

As they ambled past each stand Betty and Sara stopped to inspect the merchandise being laid out. They smiled at the men and women they encountered. Mostly young, but an occasional veteran of many seasons.

"Jesus, I thought I smelled bad sometimes," said Betty. "Can you imagine what some of these bitches are going to smell like when it gets hot later. In those gowns. I wonder if they ever clean those things."

This made Sara smile. A little Betty could go a long way. But Sara was beginning to know her as the person she really was, not the flamboyant screamer of songs. Betty was not more self-assured than anyone. She simply was more-practiced at the art of projecting an image.

"What time do you play?" asked Sara as they walked from stand to stand.

"Can you believe it? We're on at noon. Today and tomorrow. We were talking about it when we saw the schedule. This is the earliest we've ever played."

"I'm very curious how the crowd is going to react to your music. I mean, it just doesn't seem like a fit to me."

Betty nodded as they moved along.

"Here's what we've found," she said. "Here's what we know from playing out for the last couple years. Our music kind of appeals to freaks of a sort. I'm not judging. Shit, I'm about the last person in the world who should be judging anybody. But there are freaks everywhere. Of course, in big cities. They gravitate to those areas because there's comfort in numbers. But even out here in the boonies. Even with these Renaissance kids. Maybe our music doesn't fit the *theme* of this party. But it will probably fit the people here, at least a lot of them, just fine. I mean, how much lute music can you hear in a day?"

The two women strolled into the food truck area at the end of the field. They each selected a fresh drink from the juice truck and a cinnamon roll from the Bakery-On-Wheels. They sat at one of the many picnic tables adjacent to the trucks.

"I want you to know something," said Betty. "It's important, so don't interrupt me."

Sara looked at Betty's face but could not make eye-contact. Betty was staring a whole through her cinnamon roll.

"What's up?" asked Sara.

"You need to know that you're the coolest person I've ever been with," said Betty in a softer tone than Sara had ever heard her use. "I know you're not into the whole girl scene, and I respect that. I just want you to know that I hope that we'll be friends for a long time."

"We will be," said Sara. "I absolutely like being with you, Betty. We will be."

Betty sipped at her orange juice. She swallowed hard before continuing.

"Growing up where I did, in the family I had and all of that. You have no idea how hard all of that is. I was this fat girl who liked other girls. Kids at school, kids in the neighborhood, even my parents a little bit, all kind of made fun of me. So, I came out here, well, to LA. Just to see if I could be with people who were a little more open-minded. And for the most part, they aren't. They're just sneaky about it. They're just too fucking hip to be unaccepting. But you're not. You're real. And I love you for that."

Since reaching the age of ten or so, when she had outgrown the nighttime ritual of brushing her teeth and going to bed, a story and a kiss on the cheek, she had heard these words only twice. The boy with whom she'd had sex a year earlier told her that he loved her. And Pei Ling when she formally moved out of the house in Topanga. The first, a half-assed attempt to convince her that what they were about to do was justified and proper; the second, the tip of an iceberg of emotion that this woman from China had no idea how to express with any sense of completeness. Sara knew that her father loved her, but expressions of this nature did not come easily to him. Betty continued to look down.

Sara reached across the table and placed her hands over Betty's.

"I don't know what to say to that, Betty, but that made me feel really good."

"That's all I can ask for," said Betty as she looked up, smile firmly in place.

Betty Bonzo, the loud and unapologetic spokeswoman for the fringe element of humanity, was back.

Betty returned to the tour bus to meet with her bandmates before going on stage. Their routine was to run through the entire list of songs they would be performing, guitars unplugged, drums muffled. Sara stayed at the picnic table and watched people around her as they prepared for the day.

"Are you alone?"

She looked to her side to find the man who had approached without sound. He was tall, very tall, with hair as blond as her own. It fell loosely over his ears and to his collar. He wore black jeans and a black tee shirt. He was thin, resembling a distance runner. His eyes were the soft blue of robin's eggs. His demeanor was warmth, but his eyes held a fierceness and strength Sara had never encountered.

"Yes, I am," she said. "I'm here with some people, but for the moment, yes, I am alone."

He stepped to her side and towered over her, his silver belt buckle just below her eye level.

"May I join you on this fine morning?"

She was taken aback, but in an effort to appear comfortable, she motioned to the seat Betty had just occupied.

"My name is Jeff," he said. "Jeff Mist."

She took his extended hand and shook, her own hand completely engulfed by his. The man's hand was well-worn and calloused yet possessed a gentle firmness.

"I'm Sara Temple," she said.

"Very pleased to meet you, Sara. I hope you don't think this awkward or forward in any way. I just saw you sitting here on this beautiful morning and thought I'd come over and say hello."

"I was thinking it might be some sort of custom at these things, these fairs, that I just didn't know about."

Jeff Mist smiled with perfect teeth.

"Where are you and your friend visiting from, Sara?" he asked.

"LA. I'm here with this band. I mean, I'm not in the band or anything like that. A friend of mine is, and I'm kind of traveling on this tour with them. One last adventure before school starts."

"Ah…academia calls," said Jeff. "And where will you be going to school?"

"This little college not far from San Francisco. Barrow College. You know it?"

Mist shook his head.

"I don't. I've spent some time in the Bay Area, but I don't think I've ever heard of it. Not that that means a thing. Although you could say that I've pretty much dedicated my life to the acquisition of knowledge, I can't say that formal education has had a great deal to do with that."

"What do you do?" asked Sara, "if you don't mind my asking."

"I'm a Holy Man," said Jeff, answering the question almost before she had finished asking it.

She expected him to expound, to amplify on this statement with some anecdotal evidence that he was truly what he had just described himself to be. But he did not. He sat quietly and, for the first time since they had begun speaking, he stopped looking directly into her eyes.

"That's kind of interesting," said Sara after a moment of silence. "What kind of religion? If you don't mind me asking."

His smile was all-encompassing and removed every ounce of trepidation that Sara had been feeling. She was warmed by it and found an odd sense of comfort in it.

"You have to stop asking if it's okay for you to ask a question. Knowledge comes from the answers to questions. And the more questions *we* ask, as opposed to those asked by others, well, the more important the nugget of knowledge. Does that make sense?"

She nodded but did not answer.

"We practice no religion and all religions," he said. "We take from any source that might offer us an insight, a way of life that might bring us closer to God. We study, we listen, we share emotion and feelings with each other. We try to make a positive out of each day."

"What are you doing here?" asked Sara.

"We live not terribly far from here. We have a small farm. A main house, a barn, some outbuildings for work purposes. A hell of a garden, I must say. You should come visit one day. Meet the family. That sounds creepy but isn't meant to be. We all look at each other that way. That's good and bad," he added with another glowing smile.

"We're here selling some of the stuff we create at the farm. Leather goods, some carvings, necklaces and such. You should come down and meet the girls. We're halfway down the line on the right," he said pointing back up the row of stands. "They'd love to say hello."

He rose and took her hand in his.

"Go with God this morning, Sara," he said. "Let Him know you're here."

That Sara would one day find a need to explore her own spirituality was not certain. She had been raised in an agnostic household; her father considered these discussions unnecessary, and Pei Ling, never seemed to express an interest in her own beliefs, let alone ask Sara about hers. The schools that Sara had attended treated the subject as if it were child abuse. The certainty was that in the event Sara ever wandered down this avenue of thought, that her path would not be one commonly taken. She had read very little scripture in her life, had attended less than a handful of religious ceremonies of any kind, and found the dogma she suspected all organized religions to be driven by to be tedious. Even the music sucked.

As she sat at the picnic table and watched the fair come to life, she wondered if she had missed something. Could there be a piece of the puzzle that was Sara Temple that she had not known was missing?

She stood and began to walk to the tour bus where Women With No Feet would be finishing their pre-concert run-through. She wanted to time her arrival; she didn't care to hear even one more song the band had to offer. She wanted to finish this tour and get home and then off to college. More than anything, she wanted to visit the stand Jeff and his *family* operated. She was dying of curiosity to see what they were all like.

The two women were young and attractive. Neither of them wore makeup of any kind, and both had long hair loosely tied with colored ribbons. They spoke of life at the farm. They worshipped Jeff and his ability to lead them deeper and deeper into their own self-awareness. They were friendly and engaged Sara instantly.

Betty's music carried easily to where they were stationed, and Sara was embarrassed to admit that she was traveling with the band.

"They're all really nice people," she said. "They're not at all reflective of this screaming."

This made Jeff smile, and the two women sitting behind the table smiled with him.

"Sometimes we need to suffer the screaming to get to the substance," he said. "There's God's wonder in all of it, you know?"

When Betty stopped by shortly after having finished her set, Sara declined her offer to get tacos.

"I'm going to chat a little longer with Martha," she said.

After Betty had shrugged and walked quickly away, Sara returned her attention to the young woman who appeared to be the leader of Jeff's entourage. Martha wore a calf-length dress of light fabric. She sat on a folding chair, her knees slightly apart, a hand resting on each knee. Her brown hair was held in place by a blue ribbon. Her smile was made more striking by a slight imperfection in the alignment of her teeth. An orthodontist would have diminished the essence.

"You need to come for a visit," she told Sara. "We have our moments, believe me. We're not in love with each other all the time. But we have a path that is very clear to us. Jeff provides that. And we follow it. At least for the most part we do."

"Where is it?" asked Sara.

"It's a haul. But we make a loop through several states and visit a few of these festivals," said Martha.

"Well, we're leaving after the band plays their show tomorrow, so I'll probably have to take a rain check on that," said Sara. "One more concert, at an outdoor event somewhere near Reno, Nevada, and then the trip back to LA. God, I can't wait."

"Try to take a positive from it, Sara. That's what Jeff would say. That's what Jeff would say that God wants you to do. You may never see these people again, and this memory might become very precious to you one day."

"Are you people always so positive?" asked Sara with a grin. "Where have you been all of my life?"

Martha stood and walked to the card table. She opened the cash box and removed a business card.

"Here. It's our address. Send me a letter and I'll answer it. I promise."

Sara inspected the card and slid it into the back pocket of the khaki shorts she was wearing.

"What's your last name?" she asked Martha. "So that I'll know how to address the envelope."

"Just send it to Martha. There's only the one of me."

Frank Dewey Staley

Dear Martha,

I made it home to LA just in time to pack up almost all of my earthly belongings and make the long drive back up to school. Barrow is a good school, and the town is very accommodating to all of us students. Lots of pizza shops and pubs.

I would love to be able to tell you that I'm excited to begin my classes, but I'm not. I feel very much like I'm here because it's what is expected of me. When I sat and talked with you and Jeff, I was so envious that the two of you seemed so content in what you were doing with your lives. I'm only eighteen, and I get it that maybe this is some sort of passage. But the last thing I want to do is waste time. I witnessed the road you and Jeff and the others all seemed to be on…I won't use the word enlightenment…but something along those lines. And here again, I want to be envious, but I know Jeff would tell me that feeling that way would only be a waste of my energy. God, I would love to talk to him some more. Please tell him I'm trying very hard to do some of the meditation exercises he was teaching me. And please give my best regards to anyone else who might be there. How can I be missing all of you so much when I only just met you?

Please write.

Sincerely,
Sara Temple

Dear Sara,

It was wonderful to hear from you, and I'm glad that you made it safe and sound to your college. Try to make the best of it. It's a step along the journey, at least that's what Jeff would say about it.

We are all busy bees getting our canning and jarring done for the Fall. Peaches, raspberries, rhubarb, jellies and jams. We're like a pioneer family out here in the mountains. But God would not want us in a different place than this. We have moments of not having a lot to do, but Jeff always seems able to fill those with opportunities for growth.

Speaking of Jeff, he sends his love and support. He wants you to know how much he enjoyed meeting you, and he's pretty sure that you two bumping into each other is a tiny step on a master plan. I asked him if he thought it was God's will, and he said he didn't know God well enough to read His mind, but that he was going to behave as if it was His will. Jeff is remarkable. I can't begin to tell you how he has saved my life… saved me from what I was becoming before I met him.

Well, I have chores to do. Jeff bought another milk cow and now he wants to experiment with making cheese. I better run.

I hope you will find time to come see us.

Love to you from your sister,
Martha

Sara attended her classes with less than enthusiasm. Her roommate made considerable effort to engage Sara in some of the social activities enjoyed by the young women at Barrow, but with limited success.

"We're going for pizza. Emmy, that girl from the second floor and me. Why don't you come along?" said Derry.

Sara made a face and shrugged.

"I've got reading to do. And I want to get a letter off to that girl I met at that fair."

"God, Sara. It's Friday night. You have to eat, don't you?"

"Why don't you go and just bring me back a slice. I like it cold, anyway."

When Derry had attempted and failed at one last effort to lure Sara away from the dorm room, she left and headed into town with her friends.

Sara lit a candle and turned off the lights in her room. She removed the jeans and shirt she was wearing, and then her underwear and bra. Her feet were cold, so she kept her socks on. Jeff had explained to her when teaching her this meditative exercise that first afternoon at the fair, that nakedness was important. It was a strong symbol of one's closeness to God.

"Of course, you and I probably should save the naked meditation for another time," he said with a smile. "The people visiting our booth here might not understand."

She sat in the middle of the dorm room floor and crossed her legs. Her eyes closed tight, she turned her palms toward the ceiling and tried to feel starlight touching her fingertips. The boards and beams of the building were powerless to prevent the connection. Jeff had told her this, and she knew it to be true.

After many minutes of sitting, of feeling droplets of light tickling the palms of her hands, she stood and dressed. She was aware of the tears, but truly had no idea what had caused them.

Dear Martha,

Tell Jeff I'm really coming a long way with one of the meditation exercises he taught me. It's the one where you sit Indian style and try to feel rays of light touching the palms of your hands. I'm not one hundred present sure what I'm supposed to feel if I'm doing it perfectly, but I know that every time I finish, I find myself crying.

I find myself crying quite a lot. I'm so uncertain as to what I'm doing here. I'm trying. I haven't missed any classes yet, and almost everyone I know around here has missed at least a couple. It just feels like such a waste of time and energy. I learned that from Jeff. How energy is a precious commodity and that we are not to waste it. That wasting it is a sin in God's eyes. But what can I do?

I thought of just packing up my car and driving home to LA, but I know my father would go crazy. He is a wonderful man. He's done so much for me, and he raised me almost by himself...except for this Chinese woman who was kind of a live in maid/babysitter. But he's exposed me to so many different people. He just wouldn't get it if I left school. He's programmed to finish everything he starts, even if it's wasting time and energy. He just wouldn't get it.

I don't want to sound like a baby, and I don't want for you to feel like you have to put up with all my bullshit. It just changed my life when I met all of you. Jeff just opened my eyes to possibilities I didn't know existed. Please tell him that I think of him all the time and that I'm praying hard.

Love to you from your sister,
Sara

Sara meditated the following night and ended with tears and a feeling of general discomfort. Derry and the others had walked into town for coffee and pastries. Some sort of folk musician, another student there at Barrow, was playing at the coffee shop, and they were excited to hear him.

When she had finished and dressed, she sat at her desk and looked out the window across campus. It was a clear night. The place seemed deserted.

After trying to read for thirty minutes, she made the decision to join Derry and her friends in town. It was just past nine in the evening, and she knew the coffee shop would be open until at least ten or eleven.

She laced up her hiking boots and threw on a hooded sweatshirt from her high school swim team. She ran her hand through her hair, locked the door behind her and walked out into the cold air.

It had dusted snow and the frozen ground crunched beneath her boots as she walked across the open field surrounded by dorms and classroom buildings. The sky was dark, the moon and stars well-covered by clouds.

As she crossed the perimeter separating campus grounds from the town, she stayed on the sidewalk. The buildings on both sides of the narrow street were dark. Lights from the open shops three blocks ahead of her were comforting.

As she passed an open alley between buildings, she thought she heard something behind her. She turned, but before she could focus on a movement of any kind, she was grabbed and moved swiftly and forcefully into the alleyway.

Sara was not a large woman by any standard, but she was fit and strong from the athletics she had enjoyed since early childhood. But she was no match for the person holding her now. His arms encircled hers, pinning them to her sides as he walked her deeper and deeper into the darkness. She wanted to scream out, but oxygen would not find its way into her lungs. She more felt than heard herself moan. Terror was all-encompassing and paralyzed her.

"Don't worry, baby. We're just going to have a little fun," said the man in a saccharine voice. "Ain't nobody going to hurt you."

He stopped and pressed her against a wall. She felt brick against her shoulder blades and the bottom of her spine. The man was facing her. He was much taller. She didn't even make the effort to look into his face. She did not want to know what this man looked like. She only wanted to be away from him.

He placed one hand across her neck and pinned her to the wall. His other hand went to the crotch of her jeans. He rubbed her roughly. She couldn't move, more from fear than from the hold he had on her.

"What the fuck's going on here?"

The voice was loud and was different and came from the street she had just been pulled from. The man's grip on her neck gave way immediately. He stopped touching her and turned to the new voice.

"I'm just making out with my date, as if it's any of your fucking business," said the man.

Sara glanced toward the street and saw three boys, probably students returning to campus.

"Please help me," she was able to whisper. Her throat burned and her voice was hoarse.

The man stepped back from her and ran quickly down the alley. She felt herself slumping to the ground. She was not aware that the three boys helped her to her feet and walked her slowly and gingerly back to campus and into the Infirmary. Nor did she know that they each gave statements to the campus police officer who was summoned. She learned their names after having recovered from being in shock, and she made it a point to send each of them a note thanking them for helping her.

When she was asked by the on-call nurse if she would like her father notified of the incident, she stated clearly that she did not. As she was eighteen and an adult, this request had to be honored.

Dear Martha,

A man tried to rape me tonight. I was rescued by three boys who just happened to be walking by. I can't imagine what would have happened if they had not seen me. Actually, I can imagine it very clearly, and it makes me sick. It makes me wonder what I am doing here. How am I ever supposed to find my way to understanding God if I can't even be safe? I hate it here.

I hate to ask this, but could you please ask Jeff if it would be alright if I came and visited for a little while? I won't be a burden. I promise. I'll work hard. I don't know how to do anything and I'm not even very good at praying. But I'm terrified, and Jeff (and you) seem to be the only people I really trust right now.

Please let me know as soon as you can. I'm ready to leave this place.

Sara

She mailed the letter the following morning and received a response via certified mail five days later. Martha first offered her sympathy for what had happened, and championed Sara's courage for remaining strong throughout the ordeal. Of course, Jeff was delighted to welcome her to the farm. She could stay as long as she wanted. He viewed her request to come as a significant step toward knowing God. She would be safe there. She could grow and genuinely come to know herself.

Sara walked to the bookstore and purchased a book containing road maps of all fifty states and Canada. She found the town and plotted a route. Once there, she knew to get directions to the farm from the Post Office.

She returned to her dorm room and packed her clothes, her guitar and the few belongings she had brought from home. One picture of her father, another of Pei Ling. She counted the cash she had on hand and decided to wait until the following morning to leave. The bank opened at ten, and she could withdraw several thousand dollars before driving away from Barrow.

She sat one last time at the desk. Derry was not due for an hour, and she rehearsed the speech she would deliver when she returned. School not what she wanted it to be… wasting time and energy…going to stay with some friends on a farm and find herself…please don't notify anyone that I've left…when asked, act surprised. Above all, tell anyone who asks that I'm safe.

She packed her bookbag with the papers and books she felt warranted to make the trip. A deep breath. She took up pen and a notebook and began to write a letter home to her father.

Of course, Paul Danko was consulted. Sara's letter was short and very sad. She apologized for any worry she knew she would be causing her father. She was thankful for everything he and Pei Ling had done for her. But she was unsettled. The world she lived in was not the world she sought. She was not running away from anything, but towards something.

"She's an adult, Dobro," said Danko. "I mean, obviously I'm going to try to locate her. But about the only thing you can really do is call the police and report the car as stolen. It's in your name, right?"

"It is. Let me think about that. Sara's complicated, Paul. I don't know if this is a month-long gig or something more substantial. As tempting as that is, I'm not sure I want to appear that over-bearing. You're right. She's an adult."

Danko made the rounds. He visited Betty Bonzo at her new home in the valley. She was cordial and served him hot coffee but offered no insights as to where Sara might have taken herself.

"She wasn't crazy about school, I can tell you that," she said as they sat in her sparsely-furnished living room.

"Any friends I might want to talk to? Any new acquaintances?"

"When she was on tour with me, she did meet some interesting people at one of the stops. It was this massive outdoor fair with food stands and lots of people selling shit our of booths. Sara became pretty interested in these guys. They were pretty religious, but in a non-traditional kind of way. Meditation, ducking out of civilization kind of shit. But they seemed harmless, Paul. They really did."

"She spent a lot of time with them? At this fair?"

"A good amount, yeah. But I wasn't with her all that much, you know? We were...the band was rehearsing and playing our gig. Sara had a lot of spare time on her hands."

"Where was this, if I may ask," said Danko.

"I'll give you a copy of the whole itinerary," said Betty. "You can check out whatever you want. Listen, is Sara in trouble or anything like that? Or is this just another case of a rich girl *finding herself?* I think the world of her. I really do. I hope this is nothing."

Danko looked at Betty and offered a stiff smile.

"Let's hope it's just the rich girl thing," he said. "About these religious people that she met, do you have any idea where I might be able to find them?"

Betty shook her head.

"These people who sell stuff at the fairs, they're like carnival workers, but without the grunge. They travel from town to town, state to state and follow these fairs. They really could be from anywhere."

Danko handed Betty a business card as he left.

"In the event you hear from her," he said. "By the way, you have a beautiful home here."

"Thanks," she said.

She placed the card in the back pocket of the black, cut-off shorts she was wearing. She wouldn't commit to telling a soul where Sara was if Sara didn't want her location known. Danko knew this.

David Iraq refused to open the door to his house until he was certain that Paul Danko was fully convinced that no contact with Sara Temple had taken place since his visit months ago.

"She's a nice girl. But she was just a fun time. Don't be pissed at me for that. I haven't seen her since you stopped by and encouraged me not to," said Iraq.

"I'm not here for that, Mr. Iraq. Sara has kind of gone missing. Nothing nefarious. She's just taken off, and her father is very interested in knowing where she's gone. He's concerned, that's all. This has nothing to do with you. I just want to ask a couple questions."

Danko was convinced that David Iraq was telling the truth but didn't leave until he was certain that David Iraq was frightened sufficiently to call immediately upon hearing from Sara if she surfaced.

"I would be very thankful to hear from you in that event," said Paul.

"You got it," said Iraq.

When Paul Danko extended his hand to shake, the guitar player raised his own right hand as if to say, thanks, but no thanks.

The trip to Barrow was more enlightening only in that Paul Danko was able to learn that Sara had been assaulted. He interviewed Derry, as well as the three boys who had come to her aid that night. No one had any intuition as to where she might have gone.

"She wrote to this woman she met over the Summer," said Derry. "There was a bit of a religious tinge to it all. Hippy, live-off-the-land kind of stuff. But Sara never told me where she was or anything like that. I couldn't even tell you her name."

"Did Sara leave any personal things here? A notebook? Papers of any kind?"

"No, but please feel free to take a look around," said Derry.

She liked Danko. He was charming and came across as a slightly unsafe man.

"Did she know any of the three boys that helped her that night?" asked Paul.

"No. That was just pure luck."

"And the police were called?"

"The campus cops were called. I don't know if they ever caught the guy. They're campus cops, right? They handle parking tickets and kids getting drunk at football games."

Danko visited the local police and made what inquiries he could as to the incident involving Sara. The police sergeant on duty agreed to call in the event a suspect was picked up but offered no genuine sense of optimism.

"Even a hint," said Paul. "Even if you just have a twinkle of an idea that you might have someone in mind, I'd love to know."

Paul was not looking forward to telling Dobro Temple that his daughter had been the target of an assault. He could predict the response, could picture the resolve Dobro's face would assume. And he knew that Dobro would ask him to find the person who had tried to rape his daughter. To get in front of that was essential. Even if Dobro never suggested a return trip to Barrow to meet the man who had tried to rape his daughter, Paul Danko was committed to doing so.

The next many months were difficult on Dobro. He aged at a rapid rate. The pain of not-knowingness ate at him day and night.

When he had finally been told of his cancer, it came as a relief of sorts. He did not want to die. He ached to know where his daughter was, how she was, that she was safe.

But his sickness offered him something else to think about. Something different. Something other than Sara to trouble him, to keep him awake at night.

His condition worsening, he took up residence in a hospital room near Long Beach. It was no coincidence that it was closer to where Pei Ling was doing her residency. Angelica spent several hours a day with him, taking notes, making business arrangements on behalf of the clientele. The staff at The Dobro Temple Agency had all but taken over the day-to-day operation over the last two years as Dobro had slid deeper and deeper into the physical and depressive decline he was relatively certain never to come out of. But there were details to discuss, arrangements to be made, affairs to be put in order. People dying of disease are never surprised at the outcome. They can often get out in front of the details if they wish to.

"I'd like you to call this guy for me. His name is John Dudley. I don't know if you remember him, but he was the priest guy who had that radio show in Virginia. Remember Delilah Duncan? She took him under her wing."

"I remember him. That was really a weird one," said Angelica. She sat in the giant easy chair in the corner of the room, notepad on her lap.

"Anyway, he and I have stayed in touch off and on. His info is in my private file. I'd like to you give him a call and see if he can come out here for a while. Take care of tickets and stuff. He can use my car and stay at the house if he wants."

"Yes, sir," said Angelica.

She had been with Dobro from the outset and had watched his business grow from a good idea to a major player in the entertainment world. Starting as a bright-eyed surfer girl with a nice smile and a surprisingly strong work ethic, Angelica had grown to become a trusted friend of the man she worked for. He had helped her through two bad marriages, financial troubles and the deaths of both of her parents. He was a rock she could lean on, but no more so than she was for him.

She attacked these last directives with laser focus and not a small dose of love and admiration.

"Mr. Dudley? Or should I call you Father Dudley?" she asked on the phone.

"How about you call me John. And let Dobro know I'll be out there before the week's over."

Angelica greeted him at the airport, standing among the limo drivers. Her hand-made sign said *Father John Dudley.* He smiled when he saw it.

"I drove Dobro's car. He said to have you drive that, so you can drop me at the office. It's actually not that far. Unless you would prefer a hotel, he said you can stay at the house in Topanga. It's empty now."

The house will be fine," said Dudley. "But I'll need directions. I'll need them to the hospital, as well. I'd like to go there as soon as I drop you off."

John Dudley had never been a good driver. As a young man, his mother had not allowed him to drive while she was in the car. A profuse perspirer, John's hands would leave the steering wheel moist. The back of his shirt was almost always wet when he exited the driver's side.

He had never encountered traffic like that in Southern California, but it made no difference. He would have been just as daunted, just as nervous, if he had been driving a lawn mower on a golf course.

Angelica offered what advice she could on the way to the office in Santa Monica but was resigned to sitting helplessly as she watched Dudley inch along. When they had arrived at The Dobro Temple Agency, she offered to accompany him back down to Long Beach and the hospital.

"I know the area a lot better, John. I could drive and probably save you some time. Just let me grab a couple things from the office, and then we can go."

"No, but thank you, Angelica. I'll be fine. I just need to get a little more used to the traffic. Get my bearings a little. Don't be surprised, but I've never driven anywhere like this."

She was a thoughtful woman. She did not want to dent his pride by insinuating that he was incapable of handling the roadways safely. But she also didn't want him hurt. Dobro had perked up just a bit as the day of John Dudley's arrival neared, and Angelica needed him to arrive safely at the hospital. He was a disaster behind the wheel.

She nodded as if sending him on a dangerous mission in the middle of a war zone.

"Here's a map to the hospital," she said extracting two pieces of paper from her handbag and passing them through the driver side window. "It'll take you about a half hour... it'll take you about an hour and a half to get there. And then here's a map back to Dobro's place. I went out there yesterday and stocked the fridge with food and drinks. The green key on your key ring is to the sliding door on the deck."

"You've been very kind, Angelica. I have your number and will certainly call you if I need help with anything."

As he inched the car out of the parking lot and into traffic, she watched intently. When he had finally rounded the corner and had driven out of sight, she entered the building and climbed the stairs to her desk, just outside of Dobro's office on the second floor.

It was quiet, only the sounds of distant voices talking into telephones from offices down the hall. Business had slowed at the same pace that Dobro's health had deteriorated, but the other agents had done their best to assure clients that all was in order. Deals continued to be negotiated; money continued to pour into the bank accounts of the agency.

Her phone rang, and she recognized the number as coming from Dobro's hospital room.

"He's on his way," she told her boss. "He just dropped me here and left a few minutes ago."

"He's driving?" asked Dobro.

His voice sounded weak, as if there were not enough oxygen in the lungs or moisture on the vocal cords.

"I think he took it as a challenge," she said. "Don't worry, he doesn't go over twenty miles an hour, and the map I gave him takes all side streets. He should be fine."

"Well," said Dobro, his voice the timbre of exhaustion, "he *is* a priest."

"Yup," she said. "If anybody's going to make it, it's going to be him. But call me when he gets there, Dobro. Otherwise, I'll worry."

"You're a doll," he said just before hanging up.

Dobro smiled as he woke to Pei Ling's face looking down at him. She wore a red blouse under the white coat.

Dr. Pei Ling Chang embroidered in navy blue over her left clavicle.

"What's the verdict, Doctor? Am I going to pull through?" he said with a smile.

She placed her hand on his shoulder and smiled with warming light. Her schedule did not allow for daily visits, but she had come as often as she could. When she offered to see about having him transferred to the hospital she worked in, he declined.

"I don't want you bugging me every hour on the hour," he had told her.

She knew his real motivation for staying where he was; he didn't want to be a bother.

"How are you feeling today, Mr. Temple?" she asked in as clinical a voice as she could muster.

The people in the world who are near death on a regular basis recognize its footsteps as it creeps towards the dying. Pei Ling knew the outcome. She'd seen this movie many times in her brief career. And none of this prepared her for the fact that she was soon going to lose this man who had done so much for her.

"I'm feeling like a man who has cancer, I think. I guess that's the way I'm supposed to feel, right, Doctor?"

He closed his eyes. Being alert for these few seconds had tired him already. When he looked up again, it was to recognize the man entering his room. Pei Ling saw the fire flash of energy; the muscles of his cheeks and around his eyes were infused with life source. For those few moments, he was Dobro again; making deals, feet up on the desk, no socks, graying hair tousled, dress shirt with the top two buttons opened.

"There really is a God," he said as John Dudley entered the room and moved to the side of the bed opposite Pei Ling.

"Let's not get carried away," said Dudley as he took his place at Dobro's side. "The jury's still out on that one, Dobro."

"He's further gone than I was anticipating," said John in a low voice.

Dobro was out of it, barely breathing in a drug-assisted deep sleep. He and Pei Ling were sitting in his room. Dudley occupied the over-large easy chair; Pei Ling sat on a more modest folding chair extricated from the closet off to the side of the room. Light that had been flooding in through the large window was beginning to fade. Only a reading lamp standing alone on Dobro's bedside table was switched on.

She nodded. She sat with a rigid spine, her legs crossed, he hands on her knees.

"You didn't have the benefit of watching him go downhill the way we did. His cancer is very far along. I'm glad you got here when you did."

"He's done so much for me," said Dudley.

"Join the crowd," said Pei Ling.

In the hour that unfolded before them, they shared their lives with each other, the common thread being the dying man in the room.

"I was a priest. I tried to kill myself and they put me in this psych hospital. One of Dobro's clients, this rock and roll girl named Delilah Duncan took me under her wing. She saved me, really. With Dobro's help for sure."

"I noticed the scars on your wrists. Dobro mentioned you a couple of times over the years."

"We…well, *he* …stayed in touch. He'd call a couple times a year just to see how I was doing. How the show was doing. After Delilah passed away, he asked me to run her foundation. Apparently, she left a lot of money that she wanted given to the right kind of people and she figured I might be the right person to do that. In all honesty, I think she set up the radio show and the foundation just to keep me busy. But the foundation's fun and it only meets a few times a year. And I get paid, so there's that."

"I think I knew about the foundation, but what about the show?" asked Pei Ling.

Dudley laughed.

"Yeah. This Delilah Duncan, she set it all up through Dobro. She took us in. Me and this Panamanian woman who was also a suicide attempt and was staying at the same hospital. Anyway, Delilah took us home with her. Literally. We lived in her mansion and ran errands for her. One big, suicidal family all cohabitating under one roof. It was crazy."

"So, the show?" asked Pei Ling.

"Yeah, well Delilah thought that because of my training in seminary and all of that, that I had some insights into spirituality of a sort. And, hey, let's face it, I knew more than the average Joe out there about mental disorders. I mean, seriously?"

Dudley lifted his arms to expose the scars as evidence.

"So, she thought I should do some sort of call-in radio show. It wasn't like there weren't a bunch of them all over the place already. This was in the boonies. Lots of fire and brimstone stuff already *polluting the airwaves* as she put it. So, I did a radio show. For years. Even after Delilah passed away. She had put money aside for the show to continue.

And Dobro would call every couple months or so to see how the show was doing. I think it was a ploy just to check on me. What a nice, nice man."

"He put me through college and was very instrumental in getting me into med school," said Pei Ling as she re-crossed her legs. "I was hired to nanny his daughter, but it went so far beyond that. I'm convinced that Dobro was put on this planet to help people. He for sure helped me."

The two sat for a moment in silence, the rhythmic beeping of one of the monitoring machines the only noise in the room.

"I didn't help a little boy who I was capable of helping," said John Dudley. "I pretended I didn't know what to do, I talked myself into that, and it ended horribly."

There was another brief silence as Pei Ling processed.

"I guess you're here to help someone now, aren't you, John?" she said.

They discussed Sara and the impact her absence had had on her father. Pei Ling was supremely well educated and knew better than most the science behind various cancers. But she had also spent the first seventeen years of her life in China and refused to ignore the effect the unsettled essence of a person could have. Sara's absence, she was sure, did not cause her father to develop cancer. Of equal assuredness, however, at least in her mind, was the fact that the hole left in Dobro's life had been filled with cells that multiplied rapidly and steadily sucked his life-force out of him. White coat or no, she was positive of this.

Pei Ling gave Dudley an abridged chronicle of Sara's life. Headstrong, intelligent, charismatic, deferential and irreverent in equal portions. Betty Bonzo, David Iraq, the attempted rape at school.

"She was looking for some sort of spirituality," said Pei Ling. "We never provided much of that, her father and me, around the house. And I think she just needed that."

"How long has she been gone?" asked Dudley.

"Over a year."

"No communication of any kind?"

Pei Ling shook her head.

"This man who works for Dobro, Paul Danko, he's pretty sure that she ran off with some hippy, religious commune kind of people. He's done a lot of checking around. I think that's what he does. He checks around."

"I'm sure I'll meet him," said John.

Dobro stirred shortly after Pei Ling had left. John Dudley stood with some effort, he was a large man, and moved from the easy chair to the side of the bed.

"How you doing, Dobro?" he whispered.

"Thank you for coming out, John. I need a favor from you, and I didn't want to ask it on the phone."

"Anything," said the former priest.

"I need you to find my daughter. Paul…this man you'll meet shortly…he's tried. But I need you to use your God powers. Nothing else has worked so far, and I need your pipeline to work this out. You need to tell her that I love her."

"She knows that you love her, Dobro."

"Then, tell her that I forgive her. You know, prodigal daughter kind of shit."

Dobro was smiling as he said this. On the rare occasions that they spoke, the two men had often discussed religion and spirituality, the existence of God kind of stuff. Predictably, each conversation ended with more questions than answers. Dobro soliciting the aid of a God he was not certain existed was a sign of desperation, and Dudley knew this. But there was a sliver of humor in the request, as well. Who better to combine a cry for help with an inside joke than a man only hours away from death?

"I'm going to go out to your house for a few hours," said Dudley. "I need a shower and maybe a little sleep. The time change is weird. I've never been out of the eastern time zone before except for once to Chicago, and that doesn't really count."

"Angelica get you all set up?" asked Dobro.

His voice was weak, and his eyes seemed unable to fully focus. His skin was the color of pancake batter.

"She did. I have her number if I need anything. And I give you my word, Dobro, I will do everything in my power to locate your daughter. To locate Sara."

Dobro smiled.

"Hand me my wallet, John. Please."

Dobro asked this without opening his eyes.

When the priest had departed Dobro removed a folded piece of paper from the pocket of his wallet. He gently opened it fold by fold and held it in front of his face. He was incapable of reading it. The light was poor, and his vision had all but left him. But sight of that kind was not needed. He had read these words so many times, the machinery of his eyesight was not necessary. He knew the contents by heart.

Dear Dad,

I know you're going to be pissed that I've decided to leave school for a while, but I think this is something I really need to do. I've just been on such a crazy ride for the last year of my life. I feel I need to add some substance. I need to have some experiences that are positive and different and that will help me grow. I feel like something important is missing in my life, and this makes me sad almost every day. I've been crying a lot.

You and I have never really talked about God and all of that, but I have to tell you that it's an important piece of my life right now. And I've met some people, some really great and nice people who I think can help along this little journey that I'm starting out on.

Please don't worry about me and please don't send Mr. Danko off on some wild goose chase to find me. I feel good about what I'm doing, and I want you to feel good about it, too.

Give Pei Ling a hug for me and tell her to practice safe sex. (Inside joke...never mind.) We never said this very often, but I love you. And I'll see you when I've sorted everything out.

Sara

The letter was opened and rested on Dobro's chest when John Dudley returned to the room. The monitoring equipment had been disconnected and turned off. There was no light, no sound. At that precise moment John Dudley was the only person living who knew that his friend had died.

CHAPTER TWO

Rebecca Moon had been homeless for over four years. At least this is what she enjoyed telling people when the subject came up. Actually, she had lived in a multitude of places over this time, many of them comfortable and nicely-furnished; all of them in remote locations. Traveling nurses were beginning to become the rage in the late nineties, and she found the lifestyle appealing. Hospitals desperate for help would pay top dollar, many of them throwing in a place to live for the term of the contracts signed. As was often the case, Rebecca had been offered a permanent position in each of the last several postings she had accepted. But once a person starts moving on, once the nomadic itch to pack up and hit the restart button becomes more than a person can ignore, it then becomes easier to pack up the tents and round up the camels.

The road map indicating where she had been posted over the last four years could have been used by FBI agents to predict the travel patterns of fugitives fleeing justice.

Northern New Mexico to Montana to rural Florida and now, as she drove through the dense and dark forests, the State of Idaho. Rebecca had lived in places more remote, but none that seemed so challenging to get to. As she navigated the two-lane road carved through the mountainous terrain, she was compelled to keep her speed down. There appeared an *Elk Crossing* sign every few miles, and the skies, even in early Autumn, darkened early at that elevation and latitude.

What color the foliage had offered had faded to shades of brown and gray, and she was sorry she had missed this. Not what anyone would call an outdoorsy woman, she enjoyed nature from a distance. Seascapes were nice; swimming in the ocean unsettled her.

With slightly over one hundred miles still to drive to her new home, the light on her car's dashboard telling her to check the engine came on. She was as close to her destination as she remembered the last town behind her to be, so did her best to ignore the warning. Despite the lack of traffic, she was sure that if she broke down someone would rescue her from a chilly night of restless sleeping in her car.

Rebecca pulled into town to find the streets empty, and the one grocery store closed. There was a gas station, also closed, a hardware store and a clothing store of sorts. A house trailer sat at the far edge of town, the sign in front proclaiming it to be the Village Office. Churches sat at either end of town, St. Peter's to the east and The Final Word Baptist Church to the west.

"If you get religious all of a sudden, at least you'll have options," she said to herself.

She checked into a room at the only motel Dark Mountain offered. The place was clean but had seen better days. Shag carpeting of red and orange; wood paneling throughout. The towels and sheets were thin; hot water took forever to reach the shower head as she stood naked on the cold tiles of the bathroom floor.

She drank a bottle of red wine she had packed for the trip and ate a bag of salted peanuts as she lay in bed watching television after showering.

"You wanted out of the mainstream, you sure as shit got out of the mainstream," she said to the air in the room.

That she had begun verbalizing her thoughts more and more frequently did not bother her. She knew herself to be an uncomplicated woman, that on occasion it was simply comforting to hear her own voice. People sang in the shower after all.

The Pub opened at eight the following morning, a Sunday, and Rebecca walked the three blocks from the motel. She obeyed the sign telling her to seat herself and slid into a booth. The place was vintage mountain western, stuffed fox in the corner, the head of an antlered deer mounted on the wall. There was a pool table near the back of the room. Pool cues of different lengths stood in a large plastic garbage can, a vase of flowers absent the petals.

A man and woman, both dressed in dark green camouflage jackets, sat at the bar and drank from coffee mugs. A young woman with a red sweatshirt stood behind the bar dipping shot glasses into a sink filled with steaming water and then placing them in perfect rows on a folded towel laid out in front of her. Her hands looked red and raw.

The hood of her sweatshirt covered her hair, but Rebecca could see thick black curls leaking out the sides. No one spoke.

After what seemed a longer time than it was, the woman from behind the bar emerged and made her way over to Rebecca's booth.

"Coffee?" she asked.

"Please," said Rebecca. "Any chance you're serving breakfast this morning?"

"Yup," said the woman, the hood of her sweatshirt still pulled up over her head. "I'll get you a menu."

That the woman in the sweatshirt did not speak to her other than to ask how she wanted her eggs prepared did not bother Rebecca. As an outsider, she had taken meals in a variety of out-of-the-way diners, bars and restaurants and was more often than not surprised when those around her engaged her in conversation. That the locals didn't speak to each other, not the people at the bar, not the woman behind the bar, she found to be a bit odd.

After she had paid her bill and declined a refill on her coffee, Rebecca sidled her way out of the booth and retrieved the jacket she had placed on the seat next to her. She stepped to the bar and stood beside the camouflaged couple.

"Could I ask where the hospital is? Where the clinic is?" she said to no one in particular.

The man and woman looked at her as if she'd just asked them for money.

"You alright?" said the man. "You need to go to the clinic?"

Rebecca smiled.

"No. No. I just want to know where it is. I'm going to be working there, and I need to be there first thing in the morning. Usually there are signs, you know, those blue signs pointing the way. I just didn't see any here."

"We don't have no signs," said the man. "We should probably get some. Anyway, the clinic's on the main drag here," he said pointing in the direction opposite from which Rebecca had entered town the previous night. "Just stay straight and narrow on this road here and you'll run right into it."

"Thank you," she said as she turned to leave.

"What are you doing there?" asked the woman in the red sweatshirt.

"I'm a nurse," said Rebecca. "I'll be working here for at least the next six months."

"Well, you'll see our town in all of its glory then," said the man. "The winters here will make you crazy if you're not careful."

The gas station on the corner opposite The Pub had opened while she was eating her breakfast, so she filled her gas tank before heading out. The *check engine* light did not reappear, and this relieved her. She drove to the clinic to gauge the distance and returned to her motel. She walked to the grocery store and learned that it would not be opening until Monday morning. She was glad that she had packed several more bottles of wine for the trip; hanging out in The Pub simply to get a nice warm buzz before bed seemed a bit desperate.

She returned to her motel and stepped into the office. A woman wearing a green dress and white sweater sat on a stool behind the desk. Her hair was pulled up and pinned together into a bun that rested on top of her head. The color was somewhere on the scale between gray and birchbark. She had not been on duty when Rebecca checked in.

"Good morning," said the woman. "You must be in three."

"I am, and good morning. I'm just going to take a look at some of your pamphlets here."

"How's the room? You have everything you need?"

"I do. So, not much is open on Sundays, I take it."

The woman behind the desk smiled.

"We're all kind of bible thumpers around here," she said. "Well, certainly not all of us. Believe me, there are plenty of people around here who live, shall we say, a life…not in the Lord's light."

The literature rack in the motel office was filled with real estate flyers and coupon books for restaurants supposedly close by. Rebecca took one of each. She had brought along several books for downtime and relaxation, but she was indifferent just now, to reading any of them. Housing costs and lunch menus seemed far more interesting at the moment.

"Could I ask if you might have a map of the area?"

"No, sweetie, we sure don't. Maybe they have one at the gas station just over there," she said pointing. "You might try there."

"I will. Thank you."

"And please let me know if you need anything in three. I'm here until seven tonight."

Rebecca thanked her again and walked purposefully to the gas station. Even at mid-day, the sun was beginning to look for a resting place on the horizon; the air was beginning to cool.

Back in number three, she un-folded the road map and placed it on her bed. Although aware of the significant distances between towns this deep in the mountains, the remoteness of her new home seemed more apparent laid out in visual aid across her bedspread. The map showed no detail of her surroundings on front or back.

At six, she pulled on a cream-colored wool sweater and headed back to The Pub for her dinner. She had intentionally skipped lunch and was hungry.

She sat in the same booth and ordered a hamburger with onion rings and a glass of red wine. A handful of other diners were scattered at tables seemingly selected on the sole criteria of being as far from each other as possible. She noticed that no one seemed to be speaking to each other, at least not much.

She wasn't sure if her waitress was the same woman who brought her breakfast that morning. The hair seemed like it might be hers, the red hooded sweatshirt was gone.

After drinking another glass of wine and paying her bill, she stepped towards the door. It opened from the outside and the camouflaged couple from breakfast waited for her to step through.

"Hey, you again," said the woman in the green jacket.

"Hi," said Rebecca.

"Were you able to find the clinic?" asked the man.

"I did. Thank you," she said. "I start out there in the morning."

The couple entered the bar and left her standing on the sidewalk. It was close to dark as she walked the hundred yards back to her room. There was no traffic and no sound. The gas station had closed, and the little town seemed almost lifeless.

Rebecca grabbed another bottle of wine from a bag on the floor of the backseat of her car. Thank goodness the grocery store would be open tomorrow, she thought to herself.

She filled a plastic cup with wine and placed it on the soap shelf in her tiny bathroom. She turned the shower to full-on hot and slipped out of her clothes. The floor was cold on her feet. She checked the water temperature and waited. She sipped her wine and looked into the mirror. And she realized that the woman staring back at her was the first Black person she had seen in three full days.

She rose early the next morning and dressed for her first day at the Dark Mountain Area Clinic. These introductory days on a new job were never negotiated smoothly by Rebecca. She loved the work, but it was a chore to keep smiling as she was led from office to office, department to department.

"What do you think of our little facility here?"

This was from Howard Straz, the clinic administrator. He wore brown, wrinkle-free slacks and a short-sleeved white shirt. His tie was burgundy, the tip of the thin end hanging well beneath the tip of the wide.

"It is small," said Rebecca. "The agency didn't lie about that. How many beds?""

"Six, but in a pinch we can handle more. There was a bad car accident several years ago. We were already at maximum capacity but had to take in four young people who were pretty damaged. We handled it."

"And you handle pretty much everything. That's what the agency told me."

"Well, we handle what we can. We cover an area close to two thousand square miles. We can do x-rays, some very minor surgeries if needed…appendectomies, gall bladders. C-sections of course. But only in emergencies. We don't have a board certified surgeon on staff. But our doctors do what they need to do if we don't have time to transport."

"How far away is the closest full service facility?" asked Rebecca.

"Did you come in from the east or west?"

She looked up and to the left.

"From the east. Two nights ago."

"Well, if you back track all the way to the interstate and then keep going west, you'll run into a big hospital in Boise, about three hours away. Depending, of course, on the condition of the roads. We get a fair amount of snow around here."

"Snow doesn't bother me so much," she said. "I have four wheel drive in my car. I did a posting in Montana a couple years back. That was a lot of snow."

"You're our first visiting nurse, Rebecca. We're very, very glad to have you."

As they moved from area to area, Rebecca became aware that her new place of employment was not a hospital in the sense that she knew hospitals to be. There were no delineations of specialization. An expectant mother about to give birth could be in the room next to a deer hunter having accidentally shot himself in the foot next to an old woman receiving an oxygen treatment for a lung disease.

"What does an administrator in a place like this do?" she asked.

Straz had taken her to the cafeteria, and they were seated at one of the four tables in the shiny room. The menu was limited. He selected a chicken sandwich with potato chips, she a pre-made chef's salad.

"And is lunch always free for everyone?"

"Your meal is free. You get one per shift. We get funded from the state and a little bit from the county. We're part of the state-wide medical community, so there's money and a lot of support from that group. To answer your question, in a place this small, an administrator does a little of everything. I handle human resources, most of the accounting, pay the bills. In the winter I shovel the sidewalk out front. I've even drove the ambulance to Boise once. We bent a few rules that day, but it was necessary."

"I must say, Howard, that this is sure going to be a different experience for me. It's almost like you're an emergency room and a lower level treatment facility all in one."

"That's accurate," he said. "But I think what you're going to find is that nursing is nursing. You'll get just the same sense of satisfaction here as you have anywhere you've been. At least that's what our doctor and our other nurses have told me."

"How many other nurses, Howard?"

"Two and a half. And our doctor, Doctor Andrews, spends a fair amount of time at a facility on the rez a couple hours away. Usually one day a week, sometimes two. We also have Doctor Melon, but he's only around on rare occasions."

"An Indian reservation?"

He nodded as he placed his last chip into his mouth.

"Well, Nurse Moon. If you're finished, we can head to my office and talk about living accommodations for you."

She liked Howard. He was unimpressive and lived comfortably with that. He took pride in identifying the family members from the group photo on his desk.

"And this one here is the ball and chain," he said pointing to the woman Rebecca assumed to be his wife. The woman in the photo was taller than her husband and outweighed him by many pounds.

"Just kidding," said Straz. "I'm a very lucky man to have a bride like my Sue."

"Five kids?" asked Rebecca as she placed the frame back on Howard's desk.

"So far," he said. "Just the five so far."

One of her options was a studio apartment above a garage three miles out of town. Straz showed her pictures.

"The people who live in the house beside you are very nice folks," he said. "It's their garage. They're the landlords. To be honest with you, I'm told they can be a little nosy, but I'm sure they'll be respectful of your privacy."

The cabin Rebecca selected to be home for the next several months was more remote. Its owners were an older couple who lived in Spokane several hundred miles away, and they had used it as a hunting cabin for several years. According to Howard, they reached out to a real estate company specializing in out-of-the-way properties to see if it could be rented out. One of them was ill, and they would not be visiting it for a while.

"It's off the main road by about half a mile," said Straz. "I drove out there a couple weeks ago just to scope it out before you arrived. Don't worry, we'll keep it plowed. We need you to be able to get here when you're on call or in the event of an emergency."

The photos depicted a place brighter and more open than she would have anticipated. These small towns carved out of dense forest never seemed to be in full sunlight, and the buildings constructed in them shared that hint of dark and doom. A few miles from her were mountains soon to be covered with snow. Further out still were ski resorts soon to be crowded with visitors in bright colored winter clothing. Their days would be brilliant and cold, even if snow clouds filled the sky. But here in the wilderness, in this place that seemed an improbable spot for anyone to have located, the sky seemed never fully to expand. Mountains and treetops formed a false horizon. Days were just that little bit shorter.

Straz took her to the cabin shortly after lunch. He drove a pickup truck Rebecca guessed to be twenty years old. Rusted sections along the bottom were smeared with a coral-colored mud-like substance intended to prevent further corrosion. The driver and passenger seats consisted of a bench from door to door. There was no back seat, only a shallow space to keep a jacket, perhaps a pair of boots or a blanket for emergencies.

"What did you think of Nurse Pocker?" asked Howard Straz as he drove towards the turnoff that would lead to Rebecca's cabin. "We're looking for a red mailbox somewhere along here. Right after that will be the road to your new place. So, what about Pocker? You like him?"

"He seemed very nice. I have to tell you, Howard, that with the exception of meeting you, though, I haven't found the few people I've met here so far to be overly welcoming. I don't want to offend anybody, but that's just my first impression."

He drove for the next thirty seconds in silence, and Rebecca worried that she had said something she shouldn't have.

"There's the mailbox," he said as he slowed the truck down. "There we are," he added as he turned into the side road. A sign informing intruders that it was a private road was on the left. "Just remember your mailbox as your trigger to slow down, Rebecca. And yes, I think you're first impression is probably accurate. Those of us here in the boonies all have a kind of inferiority complex. You know, we're not as good as or as cool as the people living in cities. Give it a little time, Nurse Moon. I can tell already that people are going to warm up to you. Back to Pocker. What do you think?"

The cabin sat a hundred feet off the side road they had taken to reach it. The driveway consisted of sand and dirt and appeared to have retained scrape marks from the previous year's plowing. Howard climbed out of his truck and walked to the door.

"As I said, Rebecca, we'll keep the road plowed, so you'll maybe just have to do a little shoveling to and from your vehicle. There's probably a shovel inside, but if not, we can certainly get you one."

"I'll be fine," she said.

Straz unlocked the door and stepped aside to allow Rebecca to enter first. She found the light switch on the wall.

"Wow, that's bright," she said.

"We could do surgeries in here," said Howard.

The place had been built to capture as much light as possible, that was apparent. The window at the kitchen sink looked out over the driveway and back to the road. It seemed larger than it should have been, but this was unexpectedly pleasing to Rebecca. A sliding glass door was cut into the back wall and faced into the forest. The tree line was closer to the cabin than she would have liked, but she knew that she would get used to that. In all, the three room cabin was comfortable more than claustrophobic. And it came with the added bonus of not having a nosy landlord.

"I wonder if the sliding door lets in a draft?" she asked as they drove back towards the hospital.

"I'm guessing probably not. That place seems to have been built pretty tight," said Howard. "If it does, just roll a blanket up and lay it along the floor up against the door. That's what we do at home."

"Howard, can I ask a question?"

"Of course," he said not looking away from the road.

"Am I right to think it's odd to have a head nurse when the entire staff is made up of three full-timers?"

Howard Straz smiled widely at this.

"Pocker was a medic in the army. To my knowledge he didn't spend any time in what they call conflict areas. He was in shortly after we got out of Viet Nam. But he's all military. He carries it with him. Don't get me wrong. He's a very good nurse. Very detailed. Never misses a thing. But his demand to stay on with us was that he get the title of head nurse. Don't worry about it, Rebecca. I'm going to guess that your skill set is every bit as expansive as his. Probably more so."

She nodded.

"Did you notice the mileage from the town to the cabin road?" she asked.

"I'm sorry, but no, I didn't," he answered. "Just look for the red mailbox."

"I was thinking for when it got dark."

They parted in the parking lot back at the clinic. Rebecca declined an additional night at the motel in favor of moving into the cabin. There were linens and towels, dishes, pots and pans at her disposal, but she needed everything else.

At the grocery store she grabbed the basics. Milk, coffee, a chicken breast and can of green beans for her dinner that evening, a family-size bag of potato chips and three bottles of red wine.

She was not to start her first shift at the hospital until eight o'clock the next night, so her plan was to stay up as late as possible and sleep as deeply into the morning as she could.

"I hope you're alright with starting on the night shift," Straz had mentioned. "They're all twelve hour shifts and we rotate from the day shift to the night shift every four weeks. When we change, you get four days off. I hope that's okay with you."

"It's fine. I've never really minded working nights," she had answered. "God, that must be a nightmare working those schedules up."

"I look at it like a crossword puzzle," said Howard. "I actually enjoy it."

She gathered up her things from the motel, thanking the clerk as she handed over the room key.

"I hope you enjoyed your stay in our little town," said the woman behind the desk.

Rebecca entertained a momentary inclination to explain that she was not leaving town, that she would be working at the clinic for several months but fought it away. It was beginning to get dark, and she wanted to get back to the cabin while she could still find the mailbox. Extended conversation of any length would cost her time she did not have.

It began to rain as she pulled off the main road. She unloaded her car and put her groceries away. She opened a bottle of wine and poured herself a glass. The grocery store in town had a decent selection, heavy on the reds, which she preferred. She planned on driving to the mega-store three hours away once a month or so after she was settled. She could buy groceries in bulk and wine by the case.

She transferred her clothes from the giant suitcase she had lugged into the cabin to the chest of drawers in the bedroom. A box of personal items that had been in the trunk of her car, a couple of photos of her parents, candles and an alarm clock, finished the place off. Such as it was, it was now home. It didn't occur to her that she had performed these same steps so many times in the past several years in so many different places. That the ritual of settling into her new place and proclaiming it home was taking fewer and fewer minutes was of no concern to her. She was refining her art of the quick move.

She went to the shower and waited through the coughing and sputtering, the pipes not having been used in some time, for the flow of hot water. She took one of the towels out of the stand-up closet just outside the bathroom and placed it on the rack beside the shower. She removed her clothes, grabbed up a bottle of shampoo and stood in the hot water.

After drying herself and replacing the damp towel on the rack beside the shower, she walked naked into the kitchen for another glass of wine. It was fully dark outside, and the large glass windows reflected the image of her body as she moved from room to room. It occurred to her that she was fully exposed to the outside world as she poured more wine and stepped back towards the bedroom. But she knew that there was nothing out there; that there was no one lurking in the darkness of the woods peeking at this naked, almost forty year-old woman walking from room to room sipping wine from a juice glass.

Instead of the chicken breast, she heated a can of soup and opened a bag of potato chips for dinner. She tried to watch television, but she struggled to master the remote control to the satellite receiver. Although somewhat familiar with the technology, her rental house in Montana had been equipped with a satellite dish, she could only tune to three channels. She'd ask Straz to get an operator's manual from the owners the next time she saw him.

After watching a news channel until the stories began to repeat themselves, she opened another bottle of wine and tried to read. Rebecca Moon was accustomed to spending time alone. With the lifestyle she had fallen into, pulling up stakes and moving as much as she did, there was certain to be extended periods of isolation as new friendships were formed and developed. But on this night, she felt edgy and unable to enjoy the solitude she so often loved.

Shortly after midnight she pulled on her hiking boots and grabbed a sweater from the bedroom. She turned on the porch light and stepped out into the cold. The rain had turned to large, heavy flakes of snow that melted as they landed.

Rebecca walked to the end of her driveway and looked up and down the side road; left to the highway, right to God knows where. She turned her face to the sky and closed her eyes, the snowflakes feeling like tiny kisses as they melted on her cheeks and forehead.

Back inside, she locked the door and returned to the book she was reading. The reclining chair was old but comfortable. The reading lamp was adequate but needed a higher wattage bulb. She woke at three in the morning with a stiff neck, brushed her teeth and climbed into her bed. The complete silence and darkness made her think of space travel. Astronaut-Nurse Rebecca Moon. And she was certain that she could hear snowflakes landing gently on the ground outside her bedroom window.

Wanda Ripple was waiting for her when she arrived for work the next evening. She was young, mid-twenties or so, and wore expensive running shoes with her hospital scrubs. She seemed very physically fit and walked with a quickness that seemed to indicate a need to get someplace important and in a hurry. A multi-colored bandana, tied at the back of her neck, covered her dark hair; she chewed gum with parted lips.

"You must be Rebecca. I'm Wanda, one of your fellow-nurses," she said as Rebecca approached the nurse's station. "I'll be working this shift with you as kind of an orientation. I'm sure you've seen it all before. It's just what Straz wanted to do. Just for tonight."

"Rebecca Moon. Very pleased to meet you, Wanda. And thanks for showing me the ropes a little bit."

"C'mon," said Wanda. "I'll show you the nurse's lounge. It's luxurious beyond your wildest dreams, trust me. But it's where we keep the scrubs. If you're ever stranded here overnight, there's a couch."

Wanda was full of herself as many young people can tend to be, but Rebecca liked her openness and her willingness to pass along unvarnished opinions of the hospital staff.

"Straz is a dweeb, but he's a really nice man. Very devoted to his family."

"How do you get along with Nurse Pocker?" asked Rebecca.

"The General?" she answered. "You mean The General? He's alright, but he walks around here like he owns the place. Don't get me wrong, he pulls his weight. He won't ask anybody to do something he isn't willing to do himself. He's just kind of impressed with himself. Like a place this small needs a fucking head nurse."

Just after midnight, the women sat at a table in the cafeteria. Rebecca was glad that she had thought to pack a sandwich from home. She added a thermos to the mental list she was creating for her first big shopping trip.

"Then you have Deveraux. Debbie Deveraux. She's a part-timer; fills in during vacations and if someone gets sick. She's about a hundred years old but refuses to give it up. I think she trained under Florence Nightingale."

Rebecca smiled and sipped her coffee.

"What about our doctor," she asked. "What's he like?"

"*She's* alright. Doctor Andrews. Jillian Andrews. Came here about two years ago because her husband wanted to live out here in the boonies. Big hunter-fisherman kind of guy. Turns out, he hated it here and she was locked into staying for a couple years. I think they agreed to pay off a big piece of her med school debt or something like that. Anyway, he baled and moved back to St. Louis or wherever the hell they were from, and she stayed. At least so far. I will say, she's a good doctor. Not that I have many to compare her to. But she knows her shit."

"I'm looking forward to meeting her," said Rebecca.

"She and I don't really get along that well, "said Wanda. "We're cordial. We're professional. But that's about it."

"Can I ask why?"

"You're going to find out anyway, so I'll just cut to the chase. One of the main reasons her husband blew out of here was that he and I got caught…how shall I put this delicately…fucking. And she's the one who caught us. She was away at a conference in Denver and decided to come home a day early. She walked right in on her husband going down on me in her own bed. She stood there for a few seconds just watching. He didn't even know and just kept on going. He was probably wondering why I wasn't very responsive."

"Wow," said Rebecca. "At least I know now what subject matter to avoid when I meet her."

"I knew better. I know that. But you get crazy living out here in the middle of nowhere. You just make bad decisions. We get stranded out here some winter, you wait and see, we're all going to start cooking and eating each other."

"Why stay?" asked Rebecca. "You're young. You surely have options."

"My parents live here. My mom's health isn't great. I'm kind of stuck with that."

"That's commendable," said Rebecca. "I went through that with both of my parents not too long ago."

"They still with us?" asked Wanda as she dipped a celery stick into a jar of peanut butter.

Rebecca sighed deeply as she smoothed out her brown lunch bag on the table, her fingers running back and forth as if negotiating a Ouija Board.

"Nope. I lost my dad a few years ago, and my mom passed a few months after that. Cancer. Both of them."

"That's tough," said Wanda. "Sorry."

"Circle of life, right?" said Rebecca. "Onward and upward."

"Well," said Wanda as she rose from her chair, "back to the salt mine. C'mon, I'll show you where we keep the meds."

It was not until almost eleven the next night, when Rebecca was manning the floor by herself, that she met Jillian Andrews. Tall, thin, with black hair cut to a length just below her shoulders. White jacket with embroidered name, stethoscope necklace. All in order and as anticipated.

But the eyes grabbed Rebecca as they grabbed just about anyone who ever encountered them. Blue, not so much the color of ice, but of a deep and cold stream. Eyes the color of open water on a brilliantly sunny, Arctic morning.

"I heard that you were here," she said. "I'm so glad to meet you. We are all so pleased that you've decided to work with us, at least for a while."

Rebecca was sitting behind the high counter at the nurse's station adding treatment notes to a patient's chart. She stood and extended her hand across the countertop.

"Doctor Andrews. So nice to meet you. I'm Rebecca Moon. I'm glad you're here tonight. I have a few questions concerning patients."

"Let's get right to it then," said the woman in the white coat. "But please, call me Jillian. Or Jill. Or Jillie. We're far too small a place out here to rest on formality."

Rebecca had three patients to care for that evening. She had dispensed night-time meds and made certain that everyone was comfortable. As she and the doctor did the rounds, they spent several minutes in each room discussing what to look out for over the next several hours. Rebecca was impressed that the doctor took her time. It was approaching midnight, but there was no rush in Jillian's assessments, in her questions or answers.

None of the patients were deemed to be in life-threatening conditions. They would most certainly have been transported to the large hospital in Boise had that been the case. But there were still things to pay attention to. A boy with a minor concussion needed hourly observation, an old man on an antibiotic drip battling an ugly infection needed vitals taken and recorded, a woman with weak bones and white hair struggling with the flu needed oxygen treatments and at least two more bags of hydrating saline solution. Nothing Rebecca had not handled a thousand times. But being the only person in the building was a new sensation. She was not relieved when Jillian left for home and a few hours of sleep.

"I'll probably see you before you get off in the morning," said the doctor as she grabbed her bag and prepared to leave. "I can tell already that you're going to be a great asset to this place. You seem extremely capable, Rebecca."

"Well, nothing I haven't seen before," said Rebecca. "Pretty much standard operating procedure."

"From your mouth to God's ear," said the doctor. "Let's hope for that, right?"

Henry Pocker showed up at a few minutes before eight the next morning. He was dressed in navy blue scrubs and wore a pair of clogs. His mustache was unruly, but his hair was combed neatly, held in place by a gel of some sort. He was not a large man but carried himself in a manner that suggested that he wanted to be a large man. His chest seemed unnaturally extended, his shoulders drawn back, arms never fully straightened at the elbows, apparently flexing of the biceps.

"Good morning, Nurse Moon," he said as he joined her at the nurse's station. "How was your evening?"

"Please call me Rebecca," she said. "We had a good night. Doctor Andrews stopped in just before midnight and we did the rounds. I think she wanted to make sure I was okay. That was nice of her. Anyway, everyone's doing well. The man in two seems to be improving. Fever down and all of that. The kid in three had an uneventful night. Slept through vitals, but was responsive when I woke him for Q and A. The woman in four seems okay. Breathing sounds a bit improved."

"Excellent work, Nurse Moon. Would you mind staying a little longer this morning until we can bring the good doctor up to speed?"

"Rebecca, please," she said. "And no, I'll be glad to hang out for a while more."

She drove along the main road and looked for the red mailbox. These first few nights of eight to eights were going to be hard. More than once she caught herself nodding as she negotiated the long and bending highway. She rolled her window halfway down and let the cold early-morning air in.

She saw the man as soon as she turned onto her road. He was walking away from the highway, towards her cabin and probably beyond.

He walked with the posture and movements of an old man. Legs bowed; shoulders slouched forward. His steps were quick, and his strides seemed long for a small man. His legs seemed disproportionately long. Rebecca guessed that he was just a few inches over five feet tall. His hair was dirty black and gray and hung in a long ponytail down his back. He wore jeans, a heavy jacket and a black cowboy hat. His boots, the type worn by serious hikers, were well-worn and dusty.

As her car approached from his right rear, she slowed her speed to match his pace.

"Good morning," she said loudly.

He turned and looked briefly at her. Without speaking, he raised his right hand in a dismissive wave, and returned his gaze to the road in front of him.

"I'm not sure where you're going, but could I give you a lift? At least as far as my cabin?"

"It ain't your cabin," he said without turning towards her.

Rebecca rolled her window up and slowly accelerated away, careful not to raise any dust. She pulled into her drive and made certain the car was locked before she entered the cabin. She hung her jacket on a hook in the wall beside the door, poured herself a large glass of wine and stood at the sink. The view led directly to the road, and she waited for the walking man to appear.

Despite the fact that she knew he was coming, she was slightly startled to see him enter her frame of vision. She suspected that there were homes, probably cabins such as her own, further into the woods, but she had no way of being fully certain. As the man walked steadily past her driveway he did not look up. She waited for him to be well past before going outside. She walked to the road and watched the man move steadily away from her until out of sight. She entertained the notion of one day driving to the end of the road simply to see what all might be back there. But the thought of being discovered by the little man with the long bent legs discomforted her. He appeared harmless, but she had no interest in testing her intuition.

The next few nights were uneventful. Rebecca's first three patients were replaced by others. An expectant mother who could not seem to shake a headache was admitted for observation; yet another old person fighting off the flu.

Mid-way through her second week the phone from the waiting area rang at the nurse's station. It was just after nine, and the floor was quiet.

"Nurse Moon," she said into the receiver.

"Yeah, hello, Nurse Moon. This is William Glass out here in the waiting room. I wonder if you could buzz me in. I cut my hand pretty good. I think I might need stitches."

Rebecca walked to the front of the building and saw the man. He was standing at the door, his left hand wrapped in a blood-soaked rag. His weight shifted from foot to foot not unlike the manner in which children signal their parents of a need to pee.

She opened the door and held it for him.

"Gosh, that doesn't look good," she said as he walked past her and into the hallway.

"I had a flat about four miles out of town. I was on my way here, to the motel. I was having a hard time getting the spare out of the well in the trunk. I'm not really sure what I got cut on, but there's something in there pretty sharp."

"Let's take a look," said Rebecca in a calm voice. "Don't worry. These things often bleed more than you think they might. Sit up here, Mr. Glass," she said motioning to an examination table.

"Could I have a glass of water?" asked the man.

"Of course, you can. Stay right here."

She returned in a moment and handed the man a plastic cup filled with water. He held it in his right hand while she slowly and very gently unwrapped his left. When she removed the last layer of cloth and the deep, three inch laceration along the side of his hand became visible, the man moaned for just an instant before passing out. Rebecca had seen this before and she was ready for it. Although the man weighed well in excess of two hundred pounds, she was able to prevent him from falling to the floor. She hugged his chest to her own and lay him very gently onto his back. The water had spilled down her leg. She kicked the plastic cup under the examination table and began to inspect his damaged hand.

A few moments later the man returned to life. Rebecca knew that there was a definite possibility of vomiting at this point, so she had placed a bed pan on the counter beside the bed. Not the perfect receptacle for this eventuality, she knew, but it was close at hand and would do in a pinch.

"Okay, William, what I need you to do right now is just breath. Long and steady breaths, okay, Mr. Glass? In a second, we're going to sit you up again and I'm going to take another look at your hand. It's not nearly as bad as you think it is."

When he had somewhat recovered, she helped him into a sitting position, legs hanging over the edge of the examination table.

"I am so sorry," he said. "That was embarrassing."

"Not at all," she said. "I've seen that a hundred times, believe me. But I'm going to make a little suggestion for you, William. I'm going to suggest you look at the wall while I take a better peek at your hand, okay? Some people just get queasy when they see blood, especially their own."

The injured man looked intently at the wall to his right as she once again removed the rag. She estimated three or four stitches.

"I'm going to call the doctor now, William. She might come in and give you a couple stitches, or she may just have you rest here, maybe get a little sleep, and then fix you up in the morning. I'm going to go call her, and then I'll be back to clean this up for you, okay?"

"Yes," he said. "Thank you. I feel like such a baby. You're very kind."

"It's a nasty little cut, William. You're not being a baby. You sit still and don't look down. I'll be right back."

When she returned several minutes later, she pushed a wheelchair in front of her.

"Take a seat," she said. "She wants me to clean your wound and, if the bleeding has stopped, she's going to come in early in the morning and give you a stitch or two. Looks like you'll be spending the night with me, you alright with that, William."

"It seems like a lot of fuss over a little cut on my hand," he said.

"Maybe. But remember that we're kind of out here in the boonies. I could stitch you if I had to, but then where would you go? How would you get there? And besides, we need to keep this cut clean. We don't want to fool around and get an infection."

"My car's still out on the highway," he said. "The guy who picked me up…thank God he came along when he did…he drove me here. He said he was going to go back and see if he could get the tire changed. What a nice young man. Anyway, I'll need to find some way to get a ride back to my car after I leave here in the morning."

"Don't worry about that," said Rebecca. "I can drive you after I get off and you're all fixed up and ready to go."

"Kindness is all around us," he said.

"If you say so," she said. "Let's get you cleaned up now."

She wheeled him into a vacant room and slowly cleaned his wound as he sat in his wheelchair, his hand extended over the sink. The bleeding had stopped, but movement of any kind would no doubt open the cut again. She wrapped the hand in gauze and placed his arm between two pillows.

"Get a little sleep if you can," she whispered. "I know it's just a little cut but getting stuck out there on that highway late at night like that can be a bit traumatizing. You're probably tired."

She checked on the man throughout the night. He slept soundly and did not move his arm once.

Jillian and Henry Pocker arrived within a few minutes of each other the next morning. Other than the episode with William Glass, it had been a quiet night for Rebecca.

"Good morning, Nurse Moon," said Pocker.

"How's the cut hand?" asked Jillian. "Who is he, by the way. Is a local?"

"I don't know. I think he said he was going to the motel. I got all his information when I admitted him last night, I registered an address, but I don't know if it's near here or not. His name's William Glass if that helps."

"Well, let me grab a cup of coffee, and then we'll take a look," said Jillian as she walked briskly towards the cafeteria.

"I used to stitch guys up all the time," said Pocker. "In combat settings, when you're the only one on the scene, you do what you have to do to save lives."

"Someone told me that you were a military man, Henry. You'll have to tell me all about it some time," said Rebecca.

Wanda had shared with Rebecca that Pocker bristled when he was addressed by his first name, that he loved being referred to as Nurse Pocker. It was childish behavior that they referred to him exclusively as Henry and both women no doubt saw it as such. But in settings such as small and remote places with such a limited cast of characters, minor amusements are often enjoyed with exaggerated enthusiasm.

When Doctor Andrews had returned with her coffee Rebecca preceded her into the room where the man with the cut hand had spent the night. He was sitting up in his bed, a table extended over his lap. Rebecca had served him a breakfast of coffee, juice and a bagel, and he had polished these off. She had spread cream cheese on his bagel and had cut it into manageable sections for him.

"Good morning," said Jillian. "I'm Doctor Andrews. I heard you got a nice little cut on your hand last night, but that Nurse Moon here took care of you."

"She was wonderful. It's probably not that bad. Did she tell you I passed out? How embarrassing."

"She did mention that, yes. Don't think anything of it. We see that a lot," said Jillian.

"It's very common," said Pocker from the doorway.

He had followed them, but remained on the periphery, one foot in the hallway. It was not unusual for the nurse beginning a shift to perform the rounds with the nurse ending a shift, but this rankled Rebecca. Although several years younger than Pocker, she knew that her experiences in the field of nursing far exceeded his.

"Hank's right," she said without looking back at him.

The cut had remained closed with only slight tracings of blood crusted at its edges.

"Nice work, Rebecca," said Jillian as she inspected the wound before applying stitches.

Seven stitches and a tetanus shot later, and William Glass was ready to leave.

"Are you sure you don't mind driving me out to my car?" he asked Rebecca. "It might not even be drivable. The man who brought me in last night… well, I told you what he said he was going to do. But we might get out there and have to come right back into town. Why don't you let me call the gas station and have them send a tow truck?"

"Mr. Glass, it's a few minutes. I have nothing to do today except sleep, and I have plenty of time for that after we check on your car. Let's just do this."

The man accepted her kindness and sat in the passenger seat as she drove back through town and out on the highway.

"How long have you worked at the hospital," he asked as she drove with hands at ten and two on the steering wheel.

"Not long," she said. "A few weeks is all."

"What did you do before that?"

"Quite a lot, actually. I'm a traveling nurse. I take assignments that usually last six months to a year. I've been all over the place. Quite a few different jobs."

"That's a lifestyle that wouldn't appeal to everyone," said the priest. "Do you have family?"

She waited a moment before answering.

"I'm alone. My parents, both sets of them, are gone."

He looked to his left and then back at the road.

"Both sets?"

"Crazy, huh?" she said with a smile. "I was adopted by my second set of parents after my first set, my biological parents, were killed in a car crash. I was little. Third grade. I don't remember as much as I think I should."

"Gosh. I'm so sorry for you. You seem so young to have lost all those people who were so important to you. But it's wonderful that you seem to have found something you love doing and that helps so many people. You're very good at what you do, in case I forgot to tell you that last night."

"I'm not that young," she said. "I'll be forty next year. Big birthday. My first parents had me later in life and my second set, the folks who adopted me, were well into their fifties when they took me in. God, I must have been a handful."

The man looked out the window and pictured the young girl, head of wild and unruly black hair, the parents already turning gray. It was a pleasing image and made him smile.

"That's where I live," she said as they passed the red mailbox. "About a half mile down that side road there. In a little cabin."

"I'm so sorry that you have to drive all this way. I really am not sure how far out my car is. Not too much farther hopefully."

The young man who had rescued William Glass the previous night had been true to his word. The brown Ford sedan was parked on the side of the road, spare tire securely in place. They found his keys under the driver's side seat.

"I couldn't even tell you that man's name or what he looked like," he said to Rebecca. "Here, let me give you my contact information," he added. "If I can ever help you in any way, please reach out to me. I'm not sure what I might be able to do for you, but please keep me in mind. I come through here on my way to sales calls once a month or so. I cover a lot of territory but would love to be able to repay your kindness."

"All in a day's work, Mr. Glass. Take care of your hand. Change the dressing every day and keep stretching it out the way Doctor Andrews showed you. Otherwise, it'll get really stiff. Even after the stitches come out."

"Bless you," he said.

"I didn't even sneeze," she said out the window as she turned her car around.

They both smiled as she pulled out and headed back towards the red mailbox.

The first big snow of the year fell throughout the night and into the next morning. Rebecca was not troubled by the fact that she might become stranded at the hospital after her shift ended. She'd worked in rural Montana and had had to curl up on a sofa in the nurse's lounge more than once.

Pocker arrived as scheduled in the morning, and Jillian Andrews pulled in shortly after. They both proclaimed the roads to be passable but challenging.

"The plows are just now getting out," said Henry. "I think they wait until the last minute sometimes just to see if they can get away with plowing only once."

"I'm scheduled to drive to the rez this afternoon," said Jillian. "I hope this stops."

"It will," said Pocker. "But probably not until tonight."

After rounds, there were only two overnight patients to discuss, Rebecca sat in the lounge and pulled on her big boots. They were fur-lined and had come with a guarantee to prevent frostbite down to many degrees below zero. She slipped into her parka and was glad she had brought gloves, one in each pocket.

As she waded to her car through the several inches of snow, she was comforted by the silence. The sun had not yet fully risen, and the combination of cold and dark and stillness comforted her. She could capture just a hint of sound from a truck somewhere off in the distance, probably plowing.

She started her car and began the task of brushing off the accumulation. A broom would have been far easier, but the scraper she had bought while in Montana worked just fine.

She found the main road to be in good shape. It had been plowed not long before she started her drive to the cabin. She had genuine concern about negotiating the side road. The last thing she wanted to do was to get stuck halfway to her cabin. Not that the walk would be daunting. She enjoyed the winter weather and could certainly use the exercise. But the thought of having to leave her car in a spot that blocked traffic that might come along later bothered her. In the end, she decided to get at least as far as the red mailbox. If her sideroad was impassable, she'd return to town and get a room at the motel.

It was slow going, but not at all bad. Her father, her second father, had taught her to drive in snow back in Illinois.

"Don't do anything quickly," he had said. "Everything in slow motion. Slow turns, slow acceleration, slow with the brakes. Got me?"

"Got you," the sixteen year-old girl had answered.

She was relieved to find her road plowed and made a mental note to thank Howard Straz for arranging this the next time she saw him. The driveway to her cabin would need some attention, but she decided to tackle that after getting some sleep.

The driveway needed nothing. It had been plowed and the walkway from her parking spot to the door of the cabin had been shoveled. Snow was still falling, and the lack of accumulation as she walked from her car to the cabin door indicated that this work had been done recently.

Rebecca stepped out of her boots and hung her heavy coat on a hook beside the door. She poured herself a glass of wine and stood at the sink watching the snow come down. If Pocker was right, and if it kept snowing until that night, driving to work might be problematic. But she decided to worry about that only when she had to. For now, another glass of wine, pajamas and bed were all that concerned her.

The sound of the truck woke her. It was almost dark outside. She guessed four o'clock or so before looking at the alarm clock.

The window in her bedroom faced out of the back of the house and into the woods. She put on her flannel robe and walked to the kitchen. The bright red truck was finishing her driveway, expertly driving forward with the plow blade up, then lowering the blade and dragging snow backwards and away from the driveway. She attempted to make out an image of the driver but could not. Whoever he was, he had certainly done this a time or two.

The truck stopped and a man in heavy boots and a dark-colored, well-worn sweatshirt emerged and walked towards the cabin. He was carrying a shovel. He did not wear gloves.

Rebecca stepped into the boots she had placed by the door and put her parka on over the robe. She stepped out into the cold evening air fully aware of the fashion statement she was about to make.

"Simple and elegant," she whispered to herself.

"Hello there," she said to the man who was walking towards her, his boots crunching the snow beneath them.

"Hi. I'm Eliot. Eliot Samuelson. I'm the guy the hospital hired to keep your road clear, as if you probably already didn't guess that."

"They mentioned that someone would be doing that. Thank you. I'm Rebecca Moon, by the way."

He nodded and continued to move towards her, shovel in hand.

"Well, Rebecca Moon, give me just a couple minutes to shovel a path to your car and I'll be on my way."

"That's so nice of you, Eliot, but really, I can do that."

"No need. Glad to do it," he said as he began shoveling.

"Well, thank you," she said. "That's nice of you."

She turned to go inside but lingered. Turning back to him she put her hands in the pockets of her coat.

"Eliot, I was going to make some coffee before I start to get ready for work tonight. Would you like to come in for a cup?"

"That sounds great," he said. "I'll just be a minute."

As he shoveled her entry-way and a path to the driver's side door of her car, she started a pot of coffee. She moved quickly to the bathroom to pee. She washed her face and hands and made a futile effort to smooth her hair before going back to the kitchen. Eliot was standing outside the door waiting for her.

"Come in, please," she said as she opened the door.

Eliot entered and immediately stepped out of his unlaced boots so as not to track snow into her kitchen. She recognized this as standard operating procedure from her time in Montana. Seeing a stranger in socks was not an intimacy, it was politeness.

"How do you like your coffee?" she asked. "Please, sit down."

He smiled.

"Just with a little milk or cream if you have some."

She poured out two mugs of coffee and added milk to each of them. She placed the mugs on the table and sat opposite him. She guessed his age at thirty. He was not a tall man, but he was long. Long legs, long arms, long fingers. His hair was the color of wheat and was tousled from wearing the hood of his sweatshirt. His eyes were some combination of blue and green.

"Thank you again for shoveling," she said. "I was very much expecting to do that part myself."

"It comes with the bid," he said. "Although I would do it for free, to be honest. But don't tell Mr. Straz that. He'll lower the bid on me."

"Our secret," she said. "How's your coffee?"

"It's good," he said. "On days that I plow, I tend to drink way too much coffee. By the time I get home I'm all jacked up."

Rebecca sipped her coffee and looked out the window. His truck was still running, parked on the road. She could see snow falling through the beams of his headlights.

"You from around here, Eliot?"

He nodded as he drank from his mug.

"I am. I spent four years traveling," he said, "I actually traveled with *The Ice Capades,* you know the skating people? I saw quite a bit of the western states and Canada. But other than that, I've been here pretty much my whole life."

"What did you do in the *Ice Capades?*" she asked.

"I was a roadie. Lugged all the shit from the moving van to the arena and back again. It wasn't a bad job, actually. And. holy hell could those people drink. And drugs? Don't even ask me about drug use.?"

"That's impressive. You're the first roadie I've ever met. I'm not sure I could live a life like that. The constant travel, I mean."

"Sure, you could. You'd be surprised what you might be able to do if you really had to."

"I'll take your word for that," she said. "I'm really not what you would call an adventurous person."

"How do you like the clinic?" he asked.

"It's small. That's for sure. But the people are very nice. They've been very welcoming, at least after they all got to know me a little."

Eliot asked about the traveling she had done. Rebecca talked about seasons and weather. There was a comfort level as they sat and sipped at their coffee. Weather can do this. It can remove pretenses and can ratchet down inhibitions. It can provide a sense of settledness. Rebecca didn't mind that her hair was a wild and unruly mess. Eliot was comfortable sock-footed. They had the snow to thank for this.

"Well, Rebecca, I'm going to get out of your hair and get back to work. I have a couple more jobs to do. Thanks for the coffee."

"Thank you for the plowing and the shoveling. I'm sure they'll be relieved to see me at work tonight."

He placed his cup in the sink and moved to the door. His feet slid effortlessly into his boots. He turned back to the table and smiled before opening the door to leave.

"Maybe I'll see you around sometime," he said.

"Yeah," she said. "I'll look forward to it."

She walked to the sink and watched him climb into his truck. She wondered about the old man she had seen on the road, if he was able to get in and out of wherever it was he lived further along the road. She thought of William Glass and hoped that he was doing the stretching therapy Jillian had told him to do.

She watched Eliot turn his truck around in her driveway and head back to the main road. She locked her front door, poured herself another cup of coffee and moved to the bathroom for a shower. With the uncertainty of the roads, she intended to give herself a little extra time for the drive into work.

As she stood in the hot water and gently washed her brown skin with a soapy sponge, she wondered if Eliot's parting comment was an invitation of sorts. Never quick on the uptake, she was often surprised to learn that men had expressed interest in her. It usually came to her after the fact and when it was too late to do anything about it.

The ride to work was uneventful. Eliot had done a good job on her side road and the huge county trucks had kept clean the main road. The parking lot at the hospital was plowed, piles of snow like parentheses at each end of the lot.

As the evening progressed the weather cleared. She walked to the main entrance regularly to check. Snow stopped falling about two in the morning, she caught a glimpse of stars at four.

She typically did not get tired while working nights, but this night she did. There were only two patients to care for, and a genuine sense of tedium began to find its way to her. She drank more coffee than usual, but really just wanted to go back to her cabin, enjoy a couple glasses of wine and crawl into bed.

She thought of Eliot as she drove home that morning. The sun had come out and the new-fallen snow was brilliantly white everywhere she looked. She wondered what he did for a living when there was nothing to plow. Maybe she'd ask him in for coffee again and learn a bit more about him. He did not strike her as a particularly interesting man, nor was he what anyone would call a looker. But he had expressive eyes and he smiled with an ease that was appealing. She guessed that he was a good guy.

The road to the cabin and her driveway were clear. She guessed that Eliot had hit them one more time sometime in the middle of the night.

"I wonder if this snow's here to stay," she said to herself as she pulled into her drive.

She almost missed the footprints as she stepped towards her door. She followed the steps that had been left in the five or so inches of snow that had fallen over the last day and a half. The steps were deep and had not been filled to any extent with new snow. This told her that they were made recently.

She traced the trail around to the back of the cabin. She had not walked around the place before and was nervous at doing so now. The tree line into the dense woods was only a matter of feet from the building. There was no open yard to speak of.

The prints led to her bedroom window and stopped. They continued on around the other side of the cabin, past the sliding door, and to the driveway out front. She attempted to trace their origin but wasn't sure if they had come from her driveway or from the road out front. Her first thought was of Eliot, but this seemed unlikely. Then it came to her. The little man walking the road. The guy with the cowboy hat and bent legs. The sneer.

She had not seen him since their first encounter, but she attributed this to her work schedule. He had not liked the fact that she was there. This was obvious.

"What the fuck is he doing staring into my bedroom?" she asked herself. "What a creepy little guy."

Before going into the cabin, she walked to the road and inspected Eliot's plowing. From her driveway to the main road was clear. She had just driven that. In the other direction, deeper into the woods and further away from the main road, the plowing had stopped. Apparently, Eliot was paid to keep her part of the road cleared and not beyond that.

She saw footprints, only one set, along the unplowed road. The prints were coming towards her place. Wherever the little man had gone, he had not yet returned.

Despite her uneasiness, Rebecca stayed with her routine. Pajamas, a couple glasses of red wine and bed. She made certain the curtains in her bedroom window were closed tightly. She wanted it as dark as possible as she slept through the morning and early afternoon. And she did not want to even consider the thought of anyone peering in and watching her sleep.

"I think someone was sneaking around my cabin the other night," said Rebecca to Wanda.

They were sitting in the lounge, Rebecca about to leave, Wanda just coming on duty.

"Way out there? That's kind of strange," said Wanda.

She was changing out of heavy boots and into the stylish running shoes she wore while working.

"How do you know?"

"When I got home yesterday morning, I saw tracks leading from the driveway around the house. Whoever went back there stopped at my bedroom window. Should I be creeped out, you think? Or might it just be that someone is messing with me?"

Wanda shrugged.

"You have a gun?"

"Oh, God, no. I wouldn't have the first idea what to do with a gun. My parents, both sets, were pretty much pacifists. They leaned pretty far left. Gun control and all that."

"It may have been someone who took a wrong turn off the highway and was just snooping around, but you never know. This is Idaho, baby," said Wanda. "We have bears and wolves and nutjobs running all over these mountains.

The woods are filled with them. Tell you what. First time we both are off for two straight, let's drive into Boise and do a little shopping. We could spend the night in a hotel. It would be fun. And maybe we could find you a little pistola to put under your pillow."

"That all sound great except the part about the gun. I think I'd do better with a softball bat."

At the end of the following week both women found themselves off for two consecutive days.

"I'll drive," said Wanda.

They arranged for a room at a hotel adjacent to the shopping mall in Boise. Several restaurants were close by for the choosing.

"Will everything be open even though it's Sunday?" asked Rebecca.

"Yeah. Should be," answered Wanda.

She was driving the big four-door pick-up truck she had bought a year earlier. It was black and shiny and negotiated the curves and climbs without difficulty.

"There are lots of religious people here, but Idaho is full of Mormons. Everybody thinks Utah is the Mormon capital of the world, and it probably is, but we have tons of them here in Idaho. I don't think they have an issue with shopping on Sunday."

"I'm not a very religious person," said Rebecca as she sat and looked out the side window. "None of my parents were. My second parents, the Moons, they went to church once in a while. But I only remember going when it was outside, like Easter service at sunrise kind of stuff. I think my first parents were, but I don't really remember."

"I'm not either. My parents were until their health started to go. I think the closer people get to the end of their lives, the less they feel they need religion. That's backwards, right? I mean, if there is a God and all of that, the closer I get to standing in front of Him…I'm praying like a crazy bitch. I'm singing to the moon at night."

This made Rebecca smile.

"Let me ask you a question," said Wanda without looking away from the road.

"Sure."

"What kind of name is Rebecca for a Black chick? It seems too mainstream. Is that too personal or insensitive? Should I not have asked that?"

"It's fine. It's just that my first set of parents were both raised by really conservative people. When my parents met and got married, they were both very professional people. My mother worked at a bank; my father was an electrician. Even though they were proud of who they were, they never really embraced the changes that were going on in the Black culture. It made sense that they would give me some white girl name like Rebecca. At least that's my memory of it. I was pretty young when they died."

"Did you get grief about it at school? When you were little? From the other Black kids?" asked Wanda.

"I got grief about everything," said Rebecca. "I was the only Black kid in any of my classes until I went to high school. The Moons were white folks. People assume that white kids in the suburbs are enlightened and well-behaved. They're not, at least a lot of them aren't."

They checked into their hotel room shortly after two, Wanda claiming the bed closest to the bathroom. The mall was only a few hundred yards away, but they decided to drive. Despite the fact that it was a Sunday, the lot was more than half full of cars.

"Want to look at a gun?" asked Wanda.

"Maybe later," said Rebecca. "I could actually use something to eat and a glass of wine."

The afternoon was enjoyable as each woman opened, inch by inch, to the other. Rebecca found Wanda to be a bit too open and unguarded with many subjects, particularly when discussing the paucity of dating options and sexual partners. But Wanda was telling her nothing she had not heard before, nothing she had not felt before.

At one of the last stops they made late in the afternoon Rebecca bought an aluminum softball bat.

"You should have gone with a gun," said Wanda. "Just because you own one, doesn't mean you have to ever use it. What are you going to do with that bat?"

"I wouldn't be able to sleep with a gun around," said Rebecca. "I'm not the pioneer woman you are, Wanda."

They returned to the hotel to freshen up before heading out to dinner. Wanda suggested a steak house, and the women enjoyed a meal of shrimp cocktails and filets. They each drank more than they were used to, and they wisely walked the football-field distance back to their hotel.

"Nobody's gonna fuck with my truck," said Wanda as they headed to the hotel. "It has an alarm so loud that it'll wake us in our room."

At Rebecca's request, they stopped the next morning at a large grocery store on the way out of town.

"I want to buy some wine. It's so expensive at that little store in town."

Her road and driveway were plowed when she returned to the cabin late Monday afternoon. She unloaded her car: the few items of clothes she had purchased, a case of wine, all reds, a new pair of running shoes for work. The softball bat was placed in the corner of the kitchen just beside the door.

She showered and dressed in sweatpants and a long-sleeve tee shirt. She stood at the kitchen sink, barefoot, looking out over her driveway to the road. When she saw the little man, she stepped to the side of the sink so as not to be visible. He had just emerged from the unplowed section of her road and was striding, head down as usual, toward the main road.

After he had traveled beyond her field of vision, she slipped her bare feet into her big boots and walked to the edge of her driveway. She walked to the place in the road where Eliot's plowing stopped. Beyond this boundary the snow was at least two feet deep. But there was a path. Not well-worn, but certainly noticeable. She had wondered if the little man had continued walking deeper into the forest as the heavy snow had fallen but had never really looked. Maybe he had a place in town. Perhaps there was family he stayed with over the winter. Now she knew, and for a reason she could not put her finger on, this made her warm. She would have a neighbor for the Winter. A gruff and unfriendly neighbor, but a neighbor, nonetheless.

Two weeks after Thanksgiving the clinic held a holiday gathering. An extra nurse was brought in from Boise and Debbie Deveraux was put on the schedule. To Howard Straz, this was one of the major social events of the year. He was a deeply religious man who adored all things Christmas. But he was also a firm believer in building morale. A good frame of mind led to better patient care, and he was determined to provide the best patient care possible.

Straz rented out a side room at The Pub and arranged for food and drinks. Cocktails would be served at six; buffet-style dinner at seven. The entire staff and many of the people who performed contract work for the clinic were invited. All were urged to bring a date. He was relentless in the days leading up to the event.

"We'll see you Saturday night, won't we, Rebecca?"

"Wouldn't miss it for the world," she answered each time he asked.

Rebecca had sipped coffee with Eliot Samuelson twice after their first meeting. She wanted to think that he'd timed his plowing to coincide with her getting ready for work but realized that this was probably a stretch. She enjoyed his company on these occasions. He was younger by several years than she was, but his easy-going nature and boyish demeanor made her smile when she thought of him.

On the evening of the big event, she showered and put on a red dress she had purchased for the occasion. She couldn't remember the last time she'd worn heels, but the occasion seemed to call for it. She'd carry them to The Pub and change out of her big boots in the parking lot before going in. She stood in front of the full length mirror attached to the bathroom door and took inventory. A bit softer, a bit more womanly, especially through the hips. But in all, still a pretty tight package. She drove to The Pub with no thought of anything resembling a romantic interlude. All the same, she knew that there was a strong possibility that Eliot would be there. And if he was, she wanted him to notice.

Straz greeted her at the entrance. He wore dark green corduroy slacks with a red, festive sweater. Rebecca had never seen him without a tie.

"Merry Christmas, Rebecca," he said as he took her coat from her.

"Merry Christmas to you, Howard. Aren't you all dressed in holiday spirit tonight?"

Straz passed her coat to a young woman he had hired for the occasion. She hung it in the makeshift cloak room, a converted closet of sorts.

"Let's go in and get you a drink," he said to Rebecca.

It was only minutes after six, but the room was full of party-goers. Rebecca did a quick scan. Wanda, Jillian, Pocker, the cafeteria woman, several people she did not know…probably contractors or dates. She did not see Eliot Samuelson, and this deflated her slightly. She accompanied Straz to the bar and ordered a glass of red wine.

"Is Mrs. Straz here tonight," she asked him.

"For sure," he answered. "We share a love for the holidays. She's been looking forward to it almost as much as I have."

"Well, it's very nice that you do this for us, Howard. I'm sure it's greatly appreciated."

Drink in hand, she made her way to where Wanda was standing. A young man with a very full, red beard stood next to her. He was dressed in a sport coat and wore a tie that appeared too tight around his throat. He may have been comfortable, but he did not project this.

"Hey, girl. Glad you made it," said Wanda as Rebecca appeared. "This is Adam. He's my date. Adam, this is my friend Rebecca. She and I work together at the clinic."

He extended his hand and shook with Rebecca. His skin was tree bark. She could tell he was going easy on the grip so as not to harm her.

"Before you ask," said Wanda, "he's an escort. I got him to come all the way out here from Boise. He's costing me a fortune."

Rebecca glanced quickly at the man. He was blushing and shaking his head. Wanda laughed loud enough to be heard throughout the room.

"I'm just kidding," she said. "He works at a mill near Idaho Falls. We kind of have this standing date, that we go to this Christmas party once a year."

"How did the two of you meet?" asked Rebecca.

"At school. I was doing my nursing thing and Adam was studying…what were you studying?"

"Mechanical Drawing," said Adam. "But I hated being cooped up. So now I work with lumber."

"Nice meeting you, Adam," said Rebecca. "Excuse me please. I'm going to mingle."

"Want to sit with us?" asked Wanda.

Rebecca nodded and headed to the bar for a refill.

As she turned to find more of her co-workers Rebecca spotted Eliot. He was standing next to Straz, and the two men were chatting. Eliot wore a pair of wool dress slacks and a shirt with no tie. His shoes were selected for comfort; they were old and well-worn. His hair was damp, and Rebecca guessed that he had not shaved in several days.

Eliot laughed at something Straz said and was now walking toward her. She sipped her wine.

"Hi there," he said. "I was hoping to see you here tonight. How are you?"

"I'm doing well, thanks. You clean up pretty good, Eliot," she added.

"Great dress," he said. "Come walk with me to the bar. I need a drink."

They did not leave each other's side for the remainder of the evening. Rebecca felt eyes on her as she and Eliot chatted, and again when they moved through the serving line of dinner options.

"I'm going with the roast beef," she said.

"Chicken," he said. "The roast beef's going to be overdone."

After dinner, and after Howard Straz had shared a few words with the party-goers, thanking each of them by name for their hard work and dedication to the clinic, Rebecca and Eliot joined Wanda and Adam in a booth in the main room of The Pub.

Conversation flowed easily between the two women and just as easily between the two men, but few words made their way diagonally. Rebecca could feel Eliot's thigh against her own but was uncertain if the extra pressure every now and then was intentional.

After one drink, Wanda pushed Adam out of the booth and followed him.

"We're off," she said. "We have a room at the motel and the meter's running. This guy here is costing me too much to just sit here and drink with the two of you."

Adam exhaled, exasperated. He looked at Eliot.

"Don't believe this shit," he said. "She's full of it."

The two men shook hands. Wanda bent at the waist and gave Rebecca a quick kiss on the cheek.

"You okay to drive?" she whispered.

Rebecca nodded.

Eliot slipped out of his seat in the booth and sat across from Rebecca.

"Are you having a good time?" he asked.

"I am. I always like seeing people I work with in social settings. I like the different perspective. I didn't get to chat with everyone I wanted to, but it was fun."

"I'm probably to blame for that. I feel like I kind of hogged you to myself all night. But you have to remember, you and Straz are really the only people I know here. You can't blame me but so much."

"And here I was thinking all along that it was the dress."

"The dress is killer," he said as he drained the last bit of bourbon from his glass.

"I want to ask you a question," he said.

"The answer's yes," said Rebecca.

After following her to her cabin and after kissing her warmly as they stood in the kitchen, and after walking her slowly to her bedroom, Eliot unzipped the back of her dress and held it as she stepped out of it.

"You're a really pretty woman," he said as she turned to face him.

"I've been thinking quite a little bit about this," she said.

"That was a lot of fun," said Eliot.

They were enjoying a moment of closeness after having recovered their breathings. Rebecca's head rested on his chest, his arm around and under her shoulders.

"I enjoyed that," she said.

"That was a lot of pressure on me, you know?" said Eliot.

She sat up slightly, leaning on one elbow.

"What do you mean? What pressure?"

He looked at the ceiling.

"You're the first Black chick I've ever been with," he said. "I mean, that was a lot of pressure. I wasn't sure I'd live up to your standards."

Rebecca sat fully up on her side of the bed.

"Are you even fucking kidding me, right now? You're making it sound like I was some kind of science experiment. God, that's a hurtful thing to say."

Eliot sat up and attempted to place his arm around her shoulders. She pushed him away.

"No, no, no," he said. "You're misunderstanding me. I find you attractive as hell. All those times sitting in your kitchen drinking coffee with you, I just wanted to bring you back here and tear your clothes off. Especially when you were wearing that bathrobe. No kidding. But I just wanted to be honest with you. You are my first Black woman. It's not like I'm working my way through a list or anything, but you are. And I was a little intimidated."

She continued to sit and stare at him.

"You're an asshole," she said finally. "It's too bad you're so cute," she added as she lay back down.

Two days later Rebecca stayed on after her shift. One of Wanda's parents, her mother she was told by Howard Straz when he arrived at seven that morning, had fallen. She was probably fine, Straz related to Rebecca, but Wanda did not want to leave her alone. A neighbor lady was able to sit with her but could not get there before eleven or so.

"I don't mind a bit," said Rebecca.

She served the three patients occupying beds their breakfast, walked from room to room with Jillian to relate any events from the previous night and chatted with the patients who seemed to enjoy this.

As promised, Wanda showed up just before noon.

"I'm so sorry," she said to Rebecca. "Thanks for covering for me."

"How's your mother?" asked Rebecca.

"She's fine. She hurt her wrist when she slipped in the kitchen this morning. I just didn't want to leave her alone. My dad's just about useless. Usually they're fine alone."

"I'm glad she's alright. Hey, I never got a chance to ask you how your date with the escort went."

"We had a blast. We always have a blast when we're together. We even talk about one of us moving closer to the other once in a while. That might be the final solution, but not for now. He's lucky he has that job…it pays quite well. And, well you see from this morning, I'm not really flexible."

"Want to do rounds real quick?" asked Rebecca

They moved from room to room, Rebecca providing what little detail she could on the condition of the patients.

They went into the lounge, Wanda to fetch something from the handbag she had hung in her locker, Rebecca to change into her boots and grab her coat.

"So, there's a nasty rumor going around that you and the snowplow guy hooked up the night of the party," said Wanda.

"God, you'd think that if there was a place where crap like that couldn't exist, that it would be this place. These people here don't even say hello to each other when they meet on the street, yet they have no problem going out of their way to pass shit like that along."

Wanda was smiling. She had struck a nerve and was enjoying the moment.

"So, did you?"

Rebecca smiled back at her.

"Maybe," she said. "And that's all I'm going to say except for the fact that all men are jerks and that I will never trust another one as long as I live."

She saw the little man walking the main road. She had only driven a mile or two. If he was headed to his place deeper in the woods, he had a long hike ahead of him. It was miles from the red mailbox. Despite his rejection of her offer to give him a ride weeks ago, she slowed the car to a crawl and lowered her window.

"Hello. Hey, we're going to the same place. Why don't you let me give you a lift?"

He did not answer but stepped quickly towards her vehicle and opened the door. She barely got the car stopped before he was sliding into the passenger seat.

The next mile was sixty seconds of uncomfortable silence. It was palpable and hung in the car like purple smoke.

"Are you unhappy that I'm staying in that cabin?" she finally asked.

"Those were my friends. I hunted with the man; the woman made me breakfast quite a lot. I have nothing against you. I am just sad that I'll never see them again. They're old and will be moving on one of these days. I don't think they'll ever be back here."

He annunciated his words with sharpness. His R's were held a bit longer than normal. Pirate speech.

"I didn't know," she said. "But I can be your friend if you like. Maybe I could make you breakfast once in a while."

The little man smiled.

"A sad story always seems to get the girls to come around," he said. "Maybe a cup of coffee."

She parked in her drive and unlocked the door to the cabin. The little man followed her in, stopping at the door to remove his boots. He slid out if his jacket and hung it on a hook in the wall. The black cowboy hat remained on his head.

Rebecca took the coffee pot and began to run water from the faucet.

"Don't be offended that I'm not having any," she said. "I just got off from work and I go to bed about now. This is my nighttime, at least for a while longer until I change to days."

"What are you having," asked the little man. He had taken a seat at the table, the same position Eliot had occupied two nights ago.

"Don't think less of me," she said, "but I often have a glass or two of wine before going to bed."

"That sounds better," he said without changing his expression.

The little man opened up noticeably half-way through his first glass of red. Rebecca was tired but was genuinely enjoying his company.

"My name is Winton Crow," he said. "Thank you for the ride and for the glass of wine."

"Wilton, I'm Rebecca Moon. It's a little weird drinking wine at this time of day, but when you're a nurse, you get used to whacky schedules."

"Moon. That could be an Indian name," he said. "you could be Rebecca Black Moon."

"It's the name of my adoptive parents. I'm not really sure where it came from. They never really talked about it."

"We will consider it an Indian name. Rebecca Black Moon," he said as he sipped from the juice glass. "It'll give you good juju."

"Tell me about yourself," said Rebecca.

She stood and walked to the counter to fetch the opened bottle.

"I was born on a reservation about a hundred miles away from here. I come from a large family, four older brothers and a little sister. We had a decent time. My dad was a pretty serious alcoholic…aren't we all?"

Rebecca wondered if that comment was directed at her but decided not to ask.

"We were all pretty educated. There were a couple of nuns who gave us our three R's. My mother made sure we went to school. She'd give you a whipping if you skipped. She was a tiny little woman, but she could handle that belt," he said with a smile.

"I got in a little trouble when I turned sixteen. Kind of got in a fight with a white boy who had a big mouth. Even though I was underage, the judge told me I could go to jail or join the Marines. It was Viet Nam time, and joining the Marines was the last thing I wanted to do. But shit happens."

He sipped once more at his wine. Wheels were spinning in his head. Rebecca would have guessed that there had not been an occasion to allow these memories to surface in a very long time.

"Did you like the Marine Corps?" she asked.

"No. When I was sent to the war, I learned that Indian boys were treated even worse than the people of your color. Not that any of us were treated with any decency. At first, I thought the white officers put us in front of everybody else because they didn't want to get shot. But then I realized that it was really because they didn't want to have to kill anybody themselves. They didn't want all that blood on their hands. But I did meet my wife there. That was a positive."

"Wow," said Rebecca. "I would never have guessed.

The little man smiled. He was becoming more profusive with each sip from his juice glass, and Rebecca was enjoying it.

"She was this beautiful Vietnamese lady. Very petite and polite. We were out-of-our heads in love with each other, so we got married. When my tour was up, I arranged for her to come back to the states with me...well, shortly after. You know, I thought the people in Nam, the other military, the

167

Vietnamese people, that they treated us a little cold. The mixed race thing. But God almighty, that was nothing like when we got back here. We were outcasts. We were lepers right out of the bible. Poor woman."

Rebecca wanted to contribute but was spellbound. She poured the last of the wine into the two glasses and sat waiting for more.

"She died in childbirth," said the little man. "She and my little daughter. They both died. We had sketchy health care on the rez back then. It's better now."

"I think the doctor I work with, Jillian Anderson, I think she works out there a couple days a week."

"It *is* better," he said. "It's not good yet, but it is better."

"Oh, Winton. I'm so sorry to hear about your wife and daughter," said Rebecca. "How awful for you."

"I dealt with it. As with most of us, it threw me into the bottle pretty good. I got in some trouble with the law. I stole some stuff and did some time. Fifty months, actually. But when I got out, I had a little insurance money waiting for me from my wife's death. I knew some folks out this way, and they turned me on to the cabin down the road. I've been here ever since, walking this road, meeting nice people like you to share a drink with."

Rebecca yawned and rubbed her eyes.

"I'm sorry," she said. "I've been up a long time."

"Let me leave you alone," he said.

He walked to the door and slipped his feet into his boots, bending at the waist as he tied the laces. He opened the door and then closed it gently after having stepped out. Not another word.

Rebecca stood and placed the juice glasses in the sink. She watched the little man stride out of her driveway and turn right towards the deeper woods. And she knew that once the snow was sufficiently melted to allow her car to negotiate the road, that she would visit Winton Crow. This fascinating and slightly forlorn person she now considered a friend.

As Winter began to inch towards a new season, she saw Winton Crow a bit more often. Whenever they were traveling in the same direction, she would slow the car and invite him in. He accepted each time, apparently trying his best to slide into his seat before she could fully stop. The little man was able, every time, to quickly remove his hat and take his seat in one smooth motion. Despite the bow-leggedness of his limbs and the ever-present stoop to his posture, he was an amazingly nimble man.

He never spoke during these rides with the exception of a perfunctory *hello* and *thank you*. If the occasion coincided with Rebecca's return home from work, she would invite him into her cabin for a glass of wine. This turned into a bottle of wine every time, but she enjoyed the company. Winton Crow had led an extraordinary life and she liked hearing about it. And she did hear about it. The moment Winton had consumed half of his first juice glass of wine, he began to speak. She was unsure whether this was due to the alcohol, or if the fourth sip of wine triggered some sense of ritual; that he was part of social rite that now allowed him to talk about himself.

She learned that his cabin farther into the woods was without electricity.

"How do you stay warm, Winton?"

"I burn wood. It's not like we have a shortage of fuel."

"Do you have running water?" she asked.

They were nearing the end of their bottle that morning, and she felt comfortable prying for a little more information.

"I got a well. One of those old-timey wells with a hand pump. It's the best water you'll ever drink."

"Can I come see you sometime when the road clears?" she asked.

"As long as you remember to bring a bottle of wine, you can come see me whenever you want to."

He smiled at this, and Rebecca made note of the fact that this was a rare occurrence.

Rebecca had two more nights to get through before she would be going to the day shift. She looked forward to the few days off she would be enjoying between work stints. Another shopping trip to the big city with Wanda was being contemplated.

She did not dislike working the night shift but always looked forward to the schedule change. Cognizant of the fact that she might need a touch more social contact, Rebecca knew when it was time to seek it out. She lived alone in a cabin in an isolated part of the country, and she knew to be on the lookout for behavioral tics or lifestyle trends that might be leading somewhere she needn't be. Settling into a work schedule that provided no real discourse with others and staying there could be problematic.

She thought of calling Eliot but fought off the urge. As the season changed, the snow had turned to a wintry mix of sleet and rain. The ground warmed slowly. Plowing was all but over for the year, and the possibility of bumping into Eliot became more and more remote. She missed chatting with him and had certainly enjoyed their one night together, but seeing him again, although certain to be enjoyable, seemed almost a waste of time to Rebecca. He was an amusement and very clearly not an investment.

She sat at the desk at the nurse station and stared at the telephone. It was just after ten at night. When it rang it startled her.

"Nurse Moon. What can I do for you?"

"This is Deputy Clark. I'm out here in the waiting room. I have someone out here who needs your help."

"I'll be right there."

Clark was dressed in dark brown trousers and a light brown collared shirt. He wore a badge on his left breast and a name tag on his right. His gun was holstered on his right hip and seemed disproportionately big.

"Are you okay?" asked Rebecca.

"It's not me," he said with a stern look. "I have someone in the car. I found her walking along the highway. She's in and out of consciousness, so I thought I should bring her here instead of to the station."

Rebecca badged back into the clinic and returned pushing a wheelchair in front of her. Clark held the main door open for her as she made her way to the side of the Deputy's vehicle. Clark stepped in front of her and opened the rear door of the police car. A woman was lying across the back seat. She was covered in a blanket that Clark had taken from his emergency kit in the trunk of the car. Her legs were curled up slightly in a facsimile of a fetal position. Rebecca could not see her face.

"Here," said Clark. "You hold the chair still and I'll see if I can't hoist her out of there."

With effort, the man was able to reach both arms into the car and slide them under the woman's shoulders and knees. He strained at lifting her in such an awkward position but was able to extricate her from the back seat and place her, more lying than sitting, into the chair.

Rebecca wheeled the woman into the waiting area and then into the clinic.

"If you wouldn't mind helping me get her up on an examination table," she said to Clark.

"Sure thing," he answered.

Once inside the clinic, Clark removed his Park Ranger hat and placed it on a table. Rebecca wondered why he had bothered to put it on in the first place but did not comment. Men and their hats.

Once the woman had been placed on the table, Rebecca took her pulse.

"Like I said, I found her walking...stumbling along, really...out on the highway. I have no idea where she could have come from. She was miles from anywhere anyone could be living out there. Thank God it's not that cold tonight. I mean, it's cold enough. But a month ago, I'm not sure she would be alive right now."

"Did she say anything?" asked Rebecca. "Did she mention what might be wrong, where she might be hurt?"

"Not word one," said Clark. "When I pulled over and walked over to where she was standing, she just kind of fell into my arms. Poor thing."

The woman was dressed in a flannel coat, a dress of sorts underneath that buttoned to the neck. She wore heavy boots, but her skin from the ankles to just below her knees had been exposed to the cold air. Rebecca was relieved that the skin was red and not white. Maybe a mild case of frostbite, but, at first glance, hopefully not much more than that.

"If you could stay here for just a moment," she said to Clark, "I'm going to go call the doctor in. If you wouldn't mind just making sure she doesn't roll off the table in the event she regains consciousness."

"Not a worry," said Clark as he moved to his position at the woman's side.

Rebecca returned in a matter of moments.

"She's on her way in," she said.

"Is this girl going to be alright?" asked the Deputy.

"I believe so, but the doctor will be able to assess that better than I can. Maybe a little frostbite. Hypothermia, for sure. And I'm going to guess that she has some pretty serious dehydration. I'm going to hook her up to an IV now. The doctor should be here in twenty minutes."

Clark patted the woman on her exposed knee.

"You get better, there, girl. I'll be back to ask you some questions when you're up and at 'em."

He removed a business card from his shirt pocket and handed it to Rebecca.

"When she's fully conscious and you and the doctor feel it's okay for me to talk to her, could you give me a call? I'd stay but I'm pretty sure I might get in your way."

"I'll call you as soon as the Doctor feels it's okay."

Jillian arrived shortly after Deputy Cark had pulled away. She parked in the slot reserved for her and took her black medical bag from the seat beside her. When she entered the examination room, Rebecca was standing over the elevated table. A bag of fluids hung on the metal framework beside the table and was seeping, drip by singular drip, steadily down the long plastic tube and into the patient's vein. The inserted needle was taped to her wrist.

"What do we have?" asked Jillian.

"It's crazy, right. Like I said on the phone, this cop just showed up with this woman unconscious in his back seat. He found her walking somewhere out on the highway. Apparently, miles from anywhere. Her vitals are pretty good. A little low on the oxygen, but her temp is good, her pulse is strong. I'm guessing her age to be early to mid-twenties. Some redness on her fingertips and nose…the usual places for frostbite. But I don't think there's any damage."

"She's sleeping more than anything else," said Jillian Andrews. "Let's just watch her for a bit. When she wakes up, we'll try to figure out how she got out there. Do you have any coffee made?"

"No, but I'll throw a pot on. Do you need to stay here, or is this something you can just leave with me? I hate to see you wreck your whole night."

"I'll stay," said Jillian. "I might nap in the lounge later, but I definitely want to be here when she wakes up. I'm curious as hell about what happened. This dress is still very damp. Let's get her into a gown."

They expertly removed the woman's clothing by rolling her side to side. When Rebecca unbuttoned the top of the woman's dress, they both saw the bruising around the pale and white neck.

Jillian touched the dark purple skin gently.

"I don't know what caused this," she said, "but it does not look like she was choked by someone's hands. No indication of fingers with the bruising. And it's so uniformed all the way around."

The two women were silent as they contemplated what they were witnessing. Rebecca had seen the results of violence as most in the medical profession had; it was not an entirely rare circumstance for Jillian to treat victims of physical abuse on her weekly visits to the clinic on the reservation. But both were silenced by the woman's bruises. She lay quietly on the table without moving. Her lips were parted only slightly as she breathed in and out. She was fragile and her body was thin. The bruises should never have been there.

"She's sitting up and drinking some hot chocolate," whispered Rebecca.

Jillian had fallen asleep on the sofa in the lounge. She stood quickly, as if she had overslept and was late for an exam. Without speaking she followed Rebecca through the hallway and into the room they had put the sleeping woman.

"Well, I'm glad to see you back among us," said Jillian as she entered the room. "How you feeling?"

The woman sipped from her mug as Jillian did a quick inventory. Light brown hair that had not been cut or trimmed in ages. Hands red from exposure. Reddened eyes from lack of sleep and crying. Slender body...too thin to be considered healthy by anyone's definition.

"I'm alright," said the woman in a weak and raspy voice. "Where am I?"

"You're in a clinic," said Jillian. "In Dark Mountain. A police officer found you out on the highway and brought you to us. I'm surprised you weren't in shock."

"Please don't make me go back," said the woman as she began to cry. "I can't do that anymore."

Jillian placed her right hand over the young woman's shoulder.

"No one is going to make you do anything," she said. "Just relax. Drink your cocoa and sleep some more. We'll talk later in the morning. You'll be fine."

The woman placed the mug on the table beside her bed. She closed her eyes, but this did not prevent tears from rolling in starts and stops down her cheeks.

"What's your name?" asked Rebecca in as gentle a voice as she could muster. "I need it for some paperwork."

"Mandy Mist," said the woman without opening her eyes. "I was Mandy Marley before all this started happening. Before everything started to turn so ugly."

Jillian and Rebecca sat facing each other at the nurse station.

"That's disturbing," said Jillian. "I've seen stuff like this at the clinic on the rez, but I don't recall anything quite like this around here."

"Maybe people just hide their domestic abuse more carefully here in town," said Rebecca.

Jillian nodded. She was very deeply in thought.

"Well, we need to call in the authorities. And I should probably call Howard. This is probably something the administrator needs to be involved in."

"If you'll call Straz, I'll call the police back. He gave me his card when he dropped her off."

When Jillian and Rebecca had been joined by Howard Straz and Deputy Clark in the clinic lounge, no one seemed to be willing to take the lead on interviewing the woman in their care.

"If we all go in there and start grilling her, she's going to shut down," said Jillian. "She's right on the edge as it is. That's the last thing she needs."

"I'll go," said Rebecca. "I'm the one she saw first when she woke up. I'm the one who's given her the most attention…in a good way…since she got here. I'll talk to her. The three of you can just stand outside her door and listen to the responses."

Clark removed a large notepad from his back pocket.

"I need to borrow a pen if I may," he said.

"Mandy, can you tell me how you came to be out on that highway?" asked Rebecca.

She had taken up a position beside the woman's bed in a folding chair. She held her hand throughout.

"I couldn't stay there any longer," said the woman. "They were just evil, the way they treated us. God doesn't want people treated that way. Like animals."

Rebecca held a deep breath for several seconds before exhaling.

"Mandy, can you tell us…can you tell me your address?"

"Route four, box eight. Harmony. I don't know the zip code."

"Okay. This might be difficult to talk about but tell me what kind of activity you were running away from. You were running away, correct?"

The woman nodded. She had not opened her eyes. Her only movement was to wipe tears from her cheeks with the corner of her top sheet.

"We were made to work, a lot of time outside without any kind of winter clothes. In the house, when we were told to clean things, do laundry and all of that, we had to be naked a lot of the time. To humble ourselves in the eyes of God. When I first got there, I kind of understood that it was God's will for your husband to be over you, to protect you by making the decisions in your life. But it changed. It became too much…"

She did her best to stifle a choking sound from deep in her throat. Again, she wiped away tears.

"But then his brother…Jeff's brother showed up and we were told that we had to obey him, too. That was wrong, and I said so. A wife should do what her husband says. It says so in the bible. But not a brother. Not him."

"Were you hit?" asked Rebecca fully aware that her questions and answers were being recorded by Deputy Clark from outside in the hallway. "Were there any forms of physical abuse?"

The woman's hand went to her neck as if to inspect the bruises by touching them.

"What caused the injuries to your neck?" asked Rebecca. "Were you choked?"

Mandy wiped again at the moisture on her cheeks. Her nose, red from the exposure to cold air, was running freely.

"A collar," she whispered. "I can understand if your husband needs to be pleasured, that it's your responsibility as a wife. But not his brother. And if you said no, you were made to wear the collar. And he did it to you, anyway."

Rebecca looked towards the door. Throughout, she had not stopped holding Mandy's hand.

"Some sort of dog collar?" she finally asked.

"Metal. Some sort of iron. It locked in the back."

"Wherever this guy is, wherever she's running from, it sounds like there might be more out there," said Deputy Clark. "I'll take a trip out there after I run this by the station chief. He'll need to know about this even before I write it up."

The four of them had reconvened in the lounge as the woman fell back into a restless sleep. Straz sat silently making notes on a pad of paper. Rebecca seemed only capable of looking at the floor, as if her head had been filled with too much evil for her neck to support.

"She'll be here for a few more days, anyway," said Jillian. "Howard, what kind of support system do we have available to us? She certainly can't go back to where she was."

"I'll do some checking," said Straz. "To be honest, this is a first. At least since I've been here."

"The rez will take her. There's a shelter on the rez. If need be, I can get her in there."

"What's the pow-wow?" said Henry Pocker as he entered the lounge.

"Good morning, Henry," said Straz. "A patient came in last night. Appears to be a victim of domestic abuse of sorts."

"Of sorts?" said Rebecca. "Jesus Christ, Howard. Really? Of sorts?"

She had never spoken to her boss in this manner. He could have been offended, or worse, angered. But his ability to empathize with the woman lying in his clinic just now was light years short of that possessed by any other woman alive. He knew this and recognized it as his own limitation.

"I'm sorry, Nurse Moon. That was very indelicate of me."

"Can somebody bring me up to speed on the details?" asked Pocker. "My shift starts shortly."

Rebecca and Jillian left the clinic together. Rebecca desperately needed a glass of wine and some sleep; Jillian wanted a shower and a change of clothes.

"Not your average day in the neighborhood, is it?" asked Jillian.

The two women were standing just outside the main entrance. The air was cold, but the sky was clear.

"Thank God that cop, Deputy Clark, found her. We could be processing a body right now, you know?"

"Getting her back to health is going to be the easy part," said Jillian. "Did you see how she looked almost malnourished?"

"I did. Yes. That poor girl. She's somebody's daughter."

"I've got some calls to make. Get some sleep, Rebecca. You did wonderful work in there last night. You need to know that."

She wanted to see Winton Crow walking in either direction as she made her way home to the cabin. She wanted someone to talk to, even if that person happened to be a strange, little Indian man wearing a big hat and dusty boots. She wanted to count the sips of red wine it would take for him to open up and share more of his life's story with her.

As she crawled into her bed, her mouth tasting of wine, she thought of the woman in the clinic. She projected the image of Deputy Clark driving up to the house where Mandy had been kept. She wondered if there were other women there subjected to the same treatment Mandy had experienced. And if so, what would happen to them. She thought briefly of Winton Crow and then, just for an instant, of Eliot before falling into a deep, dreamless sleep.

She did not see Winton on her way into the clinic the next night. She was restless and looked forward to the four-day break she was about to enjoy before her shift changed back to days. The days were clearly warming. For the first time since arriving, she thought about her position and began to contemplate whether she wanted to stay longer than the six months she had signed on for. She liked remote, but this was seriously remote.

Pocker was a touch more authoritative than usual as he sat with Rebecca and brought her up to speed on each patient she was inheriting for the night. Deputy Clark had returned earlier in the afternoon to inform the hospital administrator and Doctor Andrews of his findings at the home Mandy Mist had come from.

"He said that there was not a whole lot that they could do," Pocker told Rebecca as she started a fresh pot of coffee. "He said that there were other women out there, that they seemed 'undamaged'...that was the word he used. That they all were quiet when asked about any kind of violent behavior."

She shook her head in disgust.

"God, Henry, what else were they going to say. And why can't the police charge him with something? Those marks on her neck didn't get there by themselves."

"Don't know, Nurse Moon."

She knew that the formal term of address just employed by Pocker was a subtle reminder that he preferred to be called Nurse Pocker.

"What about the wives? Mandy told us that all the women living there were this guy's wives. They can't do anything about that?"

"I will be the last one to defend the Mormon practice of polygamy, Nurse Moon, but the fact of the matter is that it exists, and people all over this part of the country live it. For many of them it's simply a convenient device. A way to excuse their behavior."

"So, because of where we are, because this place is crawling with Mormons, the police are just going to look the other way on that? That makes no sense. It's a law. What else did he say?"

"That was pretty much it. No signs of abuse, none of the women…I think there were only two…maybe three…came screeching out of the house wanting to be rescued…his words, not mine. And Doctor Andrews made some headway on getting Mandy into the shelter on the rez."

"Thank God for that," said Rebecca. "What would we have done with her had that not been an option?"

Pocker shook his head and shrugged his shoulders.

"I don't know the protocol on that," he said.

"The protocol would probably be to send her back to the very place she ran away from. Send her back so that the husband could put that iron collar back around her neck and parade her around in front of all his other wives. That would probably be the protocol, Henry."

She walked quickly out of the lounge and stood at the nurse station desk. Her hands were trembling. She was frustrated more than angry, but she could certainly list anger among her emotions just then.

She walked to the room where Mandy was resting and looked in. The young woman was sitting up in her bed, a pillow behind her back. She was watching television and sipping from a juice box with a tiny straw.

"How are we feeling tonight?" asked Rebecca.

Mandy nodded without looking down from the television mounted on the wall.

"I'll be your nurse again tonight. Do you remember me?"

Again, the young woman nodded.

"Okay, Mandy, I'll be back around in a little bit. Buzz me if you need anything in the meantime."

"I haven't watched TV in over a year," she said as Rebecca was almost out the door. "It's sinful. That's what my husband would always say. We didn't even own one out on the farm. We didn't even own a radio."

Rebecca stepped to the side of Mandy's bed and patted her knee gently.

"Well, you can watch all you want now," she said. "I think we have about a million channels to choose from."

"Nurse Pocker," she said as she returned to the nurse station.

He was standing at the desk making his final notations on a chart before heading home. He looked up in acknowledgement.

"I'm very sorry for the way I spoke to you just now. I'm frustrated and I'm angry and I took it out on you which is inexcusable. Please forgive me."

"You forget that I was in the military, Nurse Moon. We bathed in frustration and anger and then simply washed it off. No harm done. But thank you for the apology. Not necessary but appreciated."

"Have a nice evening, Nurse Pocker. I'll take care of everything here."

"I know you will," he said just before heading out.

It was midnight when the phone from the waiting area rang at the nurse station.

"This is Nurse Moon," she said. "What can I do for you?"

"I'm here to get my wife," said the voice from the other side of the locked door.

Rebecca did her best to calm herself before answering but failed to speak in anything other than a cracked voice.

"And who might your wife be, sir?"

It was the best she could do. Her heart raced. She was sure she could feel cold blood flowing to her brain.

"You know good and damn well who it is. Her name's Mandy Mist and she's my wife. I'm here to take her home where she belongs."

Rebecca breathed deep. She looked at the door to Mandy's room and hoped she was sleeping soundly.

"Mr. Mist, I can't release Mandy. The doctor has given orders and Mandy has stated to us and to the police that she does not want to go back there. If you'd like, you can come back tomorrow morning and speak with our administrator, Howard Straz. He'll be here around eight."

"I want to speak to my wife right now," he said.

Rebecca was fully aware that she had the flexibility to allow Mandy to speak to this man. There was nothing legal preventing it, and the police, at least according to Pocker, were not going to pursue any criminal charges. But she had also seen the terror and fragility that Mandy wore on her face. That this woman could not smile spoke volumes, and Rebecca decided to honor that.

"Mr. Mist, we are not having visitors right now. If you'd like to come back tomorrow…"

"You will unlock this door immediately," said Mist in a much quieter voice. "You will allow me to speak to my wife and if she wishes to return home to her rightful place as my wife, you will release her. Am I making myself clear?"

Rebecca swallowed with some difficulty. She stood as if attempting to assume a position of strength, a sense of gravitas she had never possessed.

"Mr. Mist, I will not unlock the door. I've made your options very clear. Your wife…Mandy is in good hands, and she has made it very clear that she does not wish to see you or speak to you. You need to leave the premises immediately or I will be forced to call the police."

She waited through several seconds of silence before hanging the phone up. She walked down the hallway to the entrance to the waiting area but could see nothing through the frosted windows on each side of the door. She thought she might have detected movement, a person walking from one side of the doorway to the other. Blurs of movement like dark ghosts through the windows. She desperately wanted to open the door and look inside but knew this to be a bad idea. She stood still and breathed as lightly as she could.

It was more a slap on the other side of the door than a knock.

"Open this Goddamn door," he screamed, again slapping the door.

She felt metal in her mouth as she walked quickly back to the nurse station to call the police and Howard Straz.

Straz arrived first. Surprisingly, he was dressed for work as he normally would be. Shirt and tie, brown laced shoes.

"Are you alright?" he asked. "Our patient alright?"

"Everyone's fine," said Rebecca. "I'm sorry to have bothered you, but I figured you would want to be here when the police show up. Legal reasons and all of that."

"Did you see the husband?"

"No. I tried to look out the windows by the door to the lobby but couldn't really see anything."

"Well, there's no one out there now," said Howard. "Your car was the only one in the lot when I pulled in."

Thirty minutes later a different Deputy showed up. He listened intently to Rebecca and made notes in his notepad.

"Can you help me with what kind of car he was driving? What he looked like? Anything?" asked the deputy.

"I'm sorry. I wasn't comfortable letting him through the door, and you can't really see much through the windows. I have no doubt that he would have taken Mandy, our patient, away from here. He only left when I told him that I was calling you."

The deputy flipped his notepad closed and slid it into his back pocket.

"Well, it *is* his wife," he said. "Here, take my card. If he shows up again, please give me a call."

Rebecca accepted the card and dropped it casually on the desk in front of her.

"I'm getting quite the collection of these," she said before turning and walking toward Mandy's room.

Straz remained at the clinic for the remainder of the night. Rebecca assured him that she was okay, that he could go home and get some sleep. But he was firm in his decision not to leave her alone.

"If he comes back, he can't get in," she told Straz. "Why don't you go get some rest? I'm alright here. Really, I am."

Howard Straz ignored her and walked down the hallway to his office.

"I'll make some fresh coffee," she said to his back. "And thank you, Howard."

He did not turn but raised his hand in acknowledgement that he had just heard what she said.

The sun was shining brightly as she walked across the parking lot to her car. She had brought Nurse Pocker up to speed on the night's developments.

"Perhaps I should switch shifts with you," he said. "Just for a bit. Until all of this settles down. I know you are capable of taking care of yourself, Nurse Moon. But maybe it would be better if you were not out here by yourself. At least for a while."

"That's very thoughtful of you, Nurse Pocker, but I'll be fine. And I only have one more night until I switch, anyway."

The ride home was pleasant. The air was warming by the minute as she drove the main road and turned at the red mailbox.

From nowhere, seemingly, she saw the car appear in her rearview mirror. There was nowhere for her to turn. Even if she could have, she was not sure the road was wide enough to accommodate two vehicles. She would have had to inch by whoever this was that seemed to be following her.

She thought of attempting to make it to wherever Winton Crow's cabin was but was certain the road was not yet sufficiently passable. In the end, she realized that the only option open to her was to pull into her own driveway. She made a mental note never to leave her home without her softball bat.

Rebecca turned from the road and parked in her driveway. She did not turn the engine off. She removed her seat belt and sat waiting. Her mouth was as dry as pine needles; her heart raced.

The car that had followed her pulled to a stop behind her. She was blocked into her driveway and her only field of vision was from her mirror. She saw two men in the car, a silver four door that she guessed to be a Honda or a Toyota. The man in the driver's side stepped out and walked around the car and towards where she was parked. She checked once more to make sure her car doors were locked.

He stood outside her door and motioned for her to lower her window. She opened it an inch, her hand trembling to the point of making this simple movement difficult.

"What do you want?" she heard herself saying.

"I want you to know that I don't appreciate you calling the police on me. I'm Mandy's husband and I intend to take her home with me where she belongs."

Rebecca sat with her eyes straight ahead. She could have been driving a hundred miles an hour and not been more focused on what lay in front of her. She refused to look at Jeff Mist. She did not want him to see the fear that she was feeling, and she was sure that she was incapable of hiding it from him.

"I know what you do out there," she said without turning. "She told me. The collar, all of that."

"This is life between a husband and wife," said Mist. "You have no right to intercede. This is God's business, not yours."

"Listen," said Rebecca, "the police aren't going to do anything. At least that's the impression I get. Why don't you just go home to your other wives and leave Mandy alone?"

She knew instantly that she should not have said this. Mist tapped on her window with his fingertips. She turned for the first time and made eye contact with him. She registered the pale blue eyes, the beard, the narrow nose. It disarmed her that he was smiling. But there was viciousness and ice in his smile, and she saw that clearly.

"You have prevented me from taking my wife to her proper place beside me. This is a sin in the eyes of God, and you will be punished for it. And know this: I am the messenger of my God, and this punishment will be from my hand."

Rebecca turned away from Mist and looked straight ahead.

"Get the fuck off my property," she said.

Mist again tapped at her window before turning and walking slowly back to his own vehicle. He carefully, foot by foot, turned his car around in the small space the end of her driveway provided. Rebecca did not move until the silver car was well out of eyesight back towards the main road.

When she was sure that Mist was gone, she opened her door and moved quickly to the porch of her cabin. She fumbled with the key, her hands still shaking.

Inside, she locked the door behind her. She picked up the softball bat standing in the corner beside the door. She considered driving back to town, back to the clinic. She thought of the deputy that had arrived at the clinic that night, and of his indifference.

"He really didn't break any laws, you know?" he had said.

In the end, she made the decision to stay where she was. She drank three glasses of wine and moved to her bedroom. She slept restlessly, fully clothed and with her softball bat at her side.

Like most women and men in her profession, Rebecca had seen her share of dying and death. Old people passing quietly in their sleep after one last taste of breath, patients of all ages possessed of an unlucky assemblage of genetic material and dying from disease they had no ability to conquer; occasionally, a man or woman unable to recover from injuries sustained in an accident.

But the death Rebecca witnessed as she stepped out of her cabin and onto the porch was different. It was not clinical. It should not have been there.

The bird's head had been cut off and lay beside the body, blood visible on both wings, also detached from the body. She guessed it to be a crow or a raven but was not sure of this. She looked out over the driveway and both up and down the road, but there was no sign of anyone's presence. This had happened while she slept, and this unnerved her.

She returned to the kitchen and took a plastic garbage bag from beneath the sink. Her Winter gloves had been unused for weeks but rested on a tiny wooden ledge just above the coat pegs attached to the wall beside the door. She put them on and went back to the porch to remove the dead bird.

Once she had placed the bird in the bag and tied it closed, she put the bag in the trunk of her car. She would dispose of it in the large green dumpster on a far end of the clinic's parking lot. After locking the door to her cabin, she carried the softball bat along with her large handbag to the car and drove towards the main road.

Pocker suggested she call the police when she related the existence of the dead bird on her porch. Howard Straz was more noncommittal.

"They're just going to tell you that there's nothing they can do. About the only crime committed, other than cruelty to an animal, is trespassing. I just don't think they're going to drive all the way back out to that guy's farm to ask him if he did this."

"But he'll know that she knows it was him that did it," said Pocker.

"He knows that already. I'm sure," said Rebecca.

In the end, she decided to heed Howard's advice and do nothing.

"Just be careful, that's all. Would you like me to arrange for you to move into town? At least for a while? I could get you set up in the motel."

Rebecca shook her head.

"I've got my bat. I'll be fine."

Mandy Mist was transported to the women's shelter on the Poshone Indian Reservation that afternoon. She had told the staff at the clinic that she was without family, at least anyone that might be willing to speak to her. Jillian assured her that she would be safe at the shelter, and that the people there could help her reconnect with friends and family if that was her desire.

"They are really tied into many of the social networks throughout the state," she said. "They might eventually be able to help you with relocation, job searches…all of that. I've arranged for you to be there as long as you need to."

Mandy cried as she was wheeled out of her room and to the front door where an ambulance waited. The men and women who had provided for her care and comfort for the past two days were simply doing their jobs. But to this young woman who had courageously walked through freezing weather for many miles in an effort to free herself from of an all-encompassing fear of abuse, they had done much more. She had attached herself to them; to their words and actions and to the fact that they were her saviors. She wanted to be as far away from her husband as possible, and the shelter represented a haven safely off in the distance. But she was leaving the people who had cared for her and protected her. The attachment was unnaturally strong. But it was a connection that was certainly understandable.

Rebecca's shift that night was uneventful. Straz had told her to call in the event anything unusual occurred. She thankfully did not need to.

Wanda Ripple replaced her the next morning, and it was good for the two to catch up. Rebecca provided as much detail as she could in relating the events of the past few days. Wanda sat attentively, fully aware that Rebecca needed to unload, to tell someone other than Pocker and Howard Straz about the craziness she had just experienced. Wanda knew that her friend had to be frightened; she also suspected that Rebecca would have been reluctant to display this emotion in front of anyone other than another woman.

"Do you want to stay with me?" asked Wanda. "I mean, you'll have to put up with my crazy parents, but you'll be sleeping most of the time you're there. You could sleep in my room. We could sleep in shifts."

This made Rebecca smile. She considered the offer, imagined herself slipping in between the sheets warmed from Wanda's body. It made her think of little girl sleepovers, and this thought was pleasing.

"That's so nice of you to offer," she said. "But I'll be fine. Everybody is telling me that this bird thing was probably a one-time act of lashing out. That this guy will probably move on with his life and leave me alone. Besides, I have my bat. The one I bought on our shopping trip."

Howard Straz walked Rebecca to the main entrance under the guise of wanting to check the weather. That he had just come in from the parking lot spoke to his rather impotent effort at misdirection; she knew full well that he was concerned about her and wanted to make sure she got to her car safely.

She thanked him before striding purposefully in her big boots, softball bat in hand, to her car.

Rebecca almost cried when she saw Winton Crow walking along the main road. He was headed into town, opposite the direction she was driving. She pulled over and rolled down her car window.

"Hi, Winton. Where have you been," she called from across the road.

"Busy," he said.

"Can I pour you a glass of wine? I know it's early, but I have quite a story to tell you."

He stood motionless for several seconds before shrugging his shoulders. He looked both ways before crossing the road and climbing into her car. Wherever he had been heading could wait.

She opened a second bottle of wine and filled both glasses. This was a first, the second bottle, and spoke to the seriousness of the conversation.

"You going to beat this man with your baseball bat?" asked Winton. He was sitting at the kitchen table, his black cowboy hat tilted back slightly more than usual. More comfortable, less formal.

"It's a softball bat," she said. "And only if I have to."

"Do you think he'll come back," said Winton? "Maybe decide to kill something other than a bird? A skunk maybe? Or a dog or cat?"

She heard the smile in his voice more than saw it across his face.

"I don't know," she said. "But if he does, I'll bash his brains in."

Rebecca's words were now spoken with a slightly thickened tongue, and this made Winton smile more openly.

"You don't think I could?" she asked. "You don't think I'm capable?"

He raised his hand in an effort to calm her.

"I never said that. I'm just sitting here wondering why you're so willing to just wait on this man. You're just going to sit here with your baseball bat and hope you get a chance to use it. I'm wondering why you don't go on the offensive with this person. Why you waiting for him?"

"I told you, it's a softball bat," she said. "And what do you mean, go on the offensive?"

Winton took a long sip from his juice glass. He looked up and out the kitchen window.

"Why don't you go to where he lives? Just drive up and tell him you don't appreciate the dead bird. That bird never did any harm to any of you. Why don't you just drive up and tell him that?"

"God, I don't think I could do that. I would be terrified."

"What if I went with you?" said Winton. "What if we just drive up to this man's house and let him see that we know where he lives and that we're not afraid to come back if we have to?"

"But I would be afraid," said Rebecca. "I would be terrified."

"This man isn't any danger to you," said Winton. "If he was going to do anything, he'd have done it already. All he did was kill an innocent bird. This is schoolboy nonsense."

"How will we find where he lives?" she asked. "Oh, wait. She gave us an address when she was checked into the clinic. But it's one of those route this, box that addresses. I wouldn't know where to begin to look for it."

"You go to the post office and ask," said Winton Crow.

She was off for a few days before starting her new rotation to the day shift. These down times, when her body was attempting to adjust to new sleep rhythms, Rebecca found herself drinking more wine than she should have. It helped her sleep and now, particularly, it helped ease the state of edginess she seemed to be carrying with her wherever she went. It had been days since finding the mutilated bird on her porch, but she could not shake the feeling that something more was going to happen. The threat to punish her that Jeff Mist had made was not some bravado born of frustration. When she had glanced at him standing beside her car door, she had seen the fire in his eyes, she had sensed the fervor.

Driving out to this man's house was an act of insanity, but she had allowed Winton to talk her into it. His insights, especially after a couple glasses of wine, were becoming more accurate the longer she knew him. He was not what she might refer to as a terribly close friend exactly; but his thinking was practical and his view of life she found both intriguing and entertaining. His understanding of the ways of the world were helpful to her.

By the morning of her third day off she had almost been restored to a circadian rhythm of sleeping through the darkness and rising with the light. It was overcast and the forecast called for rain on and off throughout the day.

As Rebecca was starting a pot of coffee, she tried hard to shake the feeling of dread that stayed with her from room to room, place to place. She decided to call the trip to visit Mist off, and then changed her mind. She was frightened at what the outcome might be, but she knew that living with the unrelenting anticipation of seeing Mist again was not an option. He had infiltrated her life from sleeping to working to dreaming, and this had to be stopped.

Winton arrived at ten. She saw him standing by the car. What an odd little man that he would not knock on the door. That he would simply stand motionless in the light rain and wait for her.

They did not speak on the drive. At the main road Rebecca turned left instead of right and towards town. They were now truly in uncharted territory. Almost an hour later, after having stopped to consult the rudimentary map she had drawn herself, she turned onto an unpaved roadway, not unlike the one to her own cabin. She drove slowly, alert to her surroundings.

"This is kind of like our road," she said to Winton.

"Except it looks like the county plows it. They don't need a young, white, handsome fella with a plow and a pickup truck to come out."

This amused her, but the smile that she began to process did not reach her lips.

They passed no buildings of any sort for well over two miles. Rebecca thought of Heather walking this distance without proper clothing and in freezing weather. The sense of gloom she had felt since waking up that morning intensified the deeper she drove into nothingness. She was certain that any moment she would have to pull the car over and vomit.

The house was old and well along its path towards disrepair. There was a barn deeper in off the roadway, and a small shack of sorts off to the side. The stairs up to the porch were not level, the foundation of the old place quite probably crumbling from age and water run-off. The walls were gray, the result of not having been painted in years. They seemed to absorb the misting rain. The windows were dark. Mist's car was parked to the left.

"Just say that you know he put that bird on your porch and that this stops today," said Winton.

They were his first words since getting in the car, and they provided Rebecca no comfort. She was paralyzed with fear but knew that she had come too far now to go back. Certainly, someone in the old and dark house had seen her drive up and was watching her.

"I forgot my softball bat," she said in a voice that cracked with fear.

"You won't need it. I'll stand with you."

They opened their doors at the same time and Rebecca walked around to Winton's side of the car. They stood shoulder to shoulder, she several inches taller, despite Winton's cowboy hat.

Mist was wearing a pair of faded blue jeans and a white sweater that seemed two sizes too big for him. He stood at the edge of the porch, his hands on his hips, his bare feet firmly planted.

"Come to repent, have you?" he said.

"I've come out here to tell you that I don't want to find any more dead animals on my porch," said Rebecca.

Mist smiled without showing his teeth. His posture did not change. Rebecca looked at each of the windows of the house but could see only dark.

"I don't know what you're talking about," he said.

"You can tell me that, and that's alright," she said. "But I want you to know all of this ends right now. I know what goes on here. Mandy told me everything, and I'm willing to leave all of that alone. But she's in a better place right now and you need to accept that and leave me alone."

"What goes on here?" he asked. "What do you think goes on here?"

"She told me everything," said Rebecca.

She detected a change in Mist, a slight movement from rational to angry. She wished she had brought her bat.

"These women are my wives," he said. "God has given me the task of caring for them, of protecting them against outside influences and Satan's darkness. Sometimes that means I have to be firm with them. You can't stop that. And God will not tolerate your efforts to do so."

"It's not my intention to," said Rebecca. "I only want to tell you to leave me alone."

This last comment sounded like a frightened child despite Rebecca's attempt at bravery. She knew it and she knew that Mist knew it.

"God's will cannot be stopped," said Mist.

"How about this," said Winton.

Mist looked at the little man with quizzical eyes. He had not anticipated that the man in the cowboy hat would join the conversation.

"How about you know that people are going to be watching out for this woman. If you stay away and leave her alone, no trouble will find its way to your door. If you don't, a boatload of trouble will."

Mist stood silent for a moment. His long blond hair was darkened from the rain. His sweater looked heavy from wetness. He looked less imposing, less a threat to do anything. Rebecca surmised that if there was going to be an incident, that it would in all likelihood not be here and now. She saw Mist, for the first time, as a coward. She didn't need the bat after all.

"My God will protect me," said Mist.

"My God's are older than your God," said Winton. Then, turning to Rebecca: "Let's go. We're done here."

Rebecca did all the talking on the drive back towards her cabin. On cue, Winton opened up halfway through his first glass of wine as they sat in her kitchen.

"Do you think that worked?" she asked.

"People live in remote places for a reason. Look at you. Look at me. Sometimes it's because they want privacy. This man lives where he does because he's afraid. He hides behind this God of his and he lives in a place where no one can challenge or threaten him. You saw that. I saw you see it."

She poured more wine into the juice glasses on the table.

"Thank you for going out there with me," she said.

"You would do it for me," he said.

"I wonder how many other women are out there," said Rebecca. "Did you hear him refer to his *wives*? There must be more, right?"

Winton nodded and sipped from his glass.

"I wish we could have the cops do some sort of background check on him, you know? Who knows what might turn up? That might be the way to get social services or somebody like that to take a look in that place. What a creepy house, right?"

"You told that man that so long as he left you alone, that you were done with this."

"Yes, but there are women out there. Probably some of them against their will. Just like Mandy. What about them?"

"I don't have an answer for that," said Winton.

"I wish we'd have gotten the license plate number. Did you notice he had California plates on his car?"

"I saw that," said Winton.

"I just wish I'd have written down the license plate number," she said.

"447B127," said Winton without looking up from his glass.

"From what I can tell, she seems to be doing fine. I haven't been able to spend a great deal of time with her personally."

This was Jillian Andrews bringing Rebecca up to speed on Mandy Mist's condition. The two women were sitting in the lounge drinking cups of hot tea. The subtle class distinction between doctors and all other personnel did not exist to the extent that it often does at larger facilities. The only person at the Dark Mountain Clinic that referred to Jillian as Doctor Andrews was Pocker.

"Please tell her that I asked about her," said Rebecca. "Oh, and I drove out to that farm that she was living at."

Jillian cocked her head, one eyebrow raised.

"I'm sorry, what did you just say?"

"It's crazy, isn't it? Remember when he followed me home that day and threatened me with God-knows-what if he didn't get his wife back?"

"That was terrifying," said Jillian. "What in the world possessed you to go to where this man lives?"

"He put a dead bird on my porch. I was really scared that he might show up again. So, this little Indian man who lives on my road…he and I have chat once in a while…he tells me that I need to go to this guy's farm and confront him. To let him know that I know that he was the one who put the bird there. So, we did. Two days ago. Me and the little Indian man drove there, and I told the man, Mandy's husband, that this nonsense was going to stop, or I was going to spill my guts about all the stuff Mandy told us."

Jillian smiled. She seemed unable to close her mouth. It was as if she was watching someone juggle knives, equal parts of fascination and worry.

"I had no idea you were so intrepid, Nurse Moon. I wouldn't have done that in a million years."

"Well, I had my little Indian friend with me. God, he's been through some stuff in his life. He kind of gave the impression that this was no big deal. That driving out there and confronting that man was all in a day's work."

"So, you spoke to the man? Mandy's husband?"

"Like I said, I told him the dead bird nonsense was going to stop. He preached at me a little more, but I really would be surprised to see him again. He's probably got other women out there, more wives, and he doesn't want me screaming to the police about it. Not that they'll do a damn thing. I saw that clearly."

"Did Mandy ever tell us how many women might be out there?"

Rebecca shook her head.

"I wish we could learn something about that man. That maybe he has a criminal record or something. If the police won't interfere because he's a polygamist, maybe they'll arrest him for shoplifting. I just wish we could get something on him."

"Do you know anything about him other than his name?" asked Jillian. "Where he's from maybe?"

"No... Yes," said Rebecca. "His car's from California. I saw that. And I got his license plate number."

Jillian made a clicking sound with her tongue. She drank the last of her tea and moved to the sink to wash out her mug. It had been given to her by Wanda in a secret Santa exchange two Christmases ago. It had a picture of a potato and said *Welcome to Idaho.* That she had kept it, that she had not smashed it against a wall somewhere, was an accomplishment. Despite the odds, she always seemed to do the proper thing.

"Give me the number," she said to Rebecca without turning from the sink. "I'll give it to one of the tribal cops I know. Maybe they can dig something up."

CHAPTER THREE

John Dudley possessed the work ethic of a Caribbean Islands basket weaver. He did not shy away from work but neither did he go looking for it. It never unsettled him to leave a project unfinished from one day to the next. If someone needed a basket, he would produce it on his own time.

He surprised himself by going into Dobro's office every day. He would rise early, particularly by California standards, and make the drive along the Pacific Coast Highway from Topanga to Santa Monica. He hated the traffic in Southern California and was frightened to death of damaging Dobro's very expensive Mercedes sedan. But he learned quickly that the earlier he left the house, the lighter the traffic would be as he drove along the coast. And on mornings when the waves were good, he could see men and women surfing as he drove along. Southern California was such an odd place for him to be. It could have been another planet and not been more different than what he was used to.

He never opted to park in the slot reserved for Dobro. This would have been disrespectful of the dearly departed and a sacrilege of sorts.

Dudley could conjugate verbs in Latin but had no clue how to go about making inquiries as to the whereabouts of the lost daughter of his dead friend. He met a couple of times a week with Paul Danko, but new ideas, new tactics towards locating Sara Temple did not present themselves. Danko shared every bit of information he had assembled, offered speculations that ranged from Sara living happily-ever-after to that of her living homeless, as a prostitute or worse. But nothing solid was available. Dudley had promised his friend Dobro Temple that he would make every effort to find the girl. He simply had no inkling as to how to go about doing it.

He called Betty Bonzo. He called David Iraq. He called Barrow and spoke to the Dean of Student Affairs. But Danko had conducted these interviews in person and within a matter of weeks from the moment Sara dropped off the earth. Dudley knew full well that if Paul had been unable to glean any useful information from these discussions, that it was a stretch to think that he himself could. But it was a promise he had made; it was a basket that needed to be woven.

Once a week, usually on Saturday, he would call Pei Ling and give her the unwelcome news that he had nothing new to offer. She did her best to keep his spirits up, to provide the spark necessary for his efforts to be maintained. But these conversations ended with frustration, their voices ratcheting down the longer they spoke.

"Talk next week," each of them would say with a heavy sigh.

The first day he was visited by one of the agency's clients was like a child visiting an amusement park for the first time. John Dudley was excitedly nervous as he waited for the client Angelica had told him was coming to visit, but he didn't truly know why. In the last several months of his life Dobro had all but extricated himself from the day-to-day of the business. There were other agents on the payroll, and most of the heavy lifting, signing new endorsement deals, pushing this project or that to the proper decision maker, these tasks all had been off-loaded to them. Dobro had actually had very little contact with any of his clients, even those who had been with him for over a decade. Dobro had shared with John Dudley the fact that the agency might disappear as soon as its founder left the building for the last time but wasn't truly certain.

"I really don't know," he had whispered from his hospital bed. "But I want you to use the office. Angelica will stay. She's taken care of. There's lots of money, John. None of you have to worry at all."

Dudley waited for news that the agency was closing, but it never came. He sat in Dobro's chair and read newspapers. Each day, Angelica would order lunch for the two of them, and they would sit at the conference table in Dobro's office and chat. Dudley found her to be a genuinely warm and kind woman who considered Dobro Temple a saint and savior no less than he did.

"Did Dobro leave you in charge? Are you the man now?"

These questions came from a very handsome, very troubled-looking young man sitting across the desk from John Dudley. He was an actor who was rumored to be in the running for a role that would change his life, that would cement his position as one of the few truly sought after big names in the industry, and he was visiting the office of his agent to assess the likelihood of his landing the job.

"No," said Dudley, "I'm a close friend of Dobro's, and he asked me to handle a few things for him. I'm staying at his house and using his office while I take care of these things. But I'm delighted to meet you."

"Dude. My main agent, my rep that Dobro assigned me to, Stuart...you know Stuart? A really good guy, and he's all over this. I mean, he tells me that we're pretty sure this part is coming my way. Stuart's great. But we all miss Dobro, right?"

John Dudley tilted his large head slightly as he attempted to discern if there was something important the actor had just said. It seemed to be an assemblage of unconnected words, at least to him, but he truly wanted to give the handsome young man the benefit of the doubt.

"Indeed," said Dudley with as serious a look on his face as he could manufacture.

"So how do you know the man?" asked the actor. "How are you and my man Dobro connected?"

"We met many years ago. I used to be a priest, and Dobro got me set up with a radio show. I talked a lot about spirituality. We helped a lot of people."

The entertainment industry, particularly that portion of its participants living in Los Angeles, included many rational and pragmatic thinkers. The actor sitting across the desk from Dudley that morning was not one of them. He interpreted the fact that John Dudley had once been a priest as a clear message from whatever peyote-infused, crystal jewelry-wearing source of intelligence he prayed to. And the message reached him, as it began to reach several other clients of the Dobro Temple Agency as they came to understand that Dobro had left matters in the hands of someone capable of handling the almost mystical demands of representing them. Friends and acquaintances of the agency's clientele had gurus, they had Yoga Instructors, they had men and women in sandals who wore beads around their necks. Dobro's people had a priest. Dudley became Oz-like as he gave audiences to the men and women who had learned of his ascension. On days when he allowed it, he felt like the pope.

"You have to understand that this is Los Angeles," said Angelica. "So many people move here because they're just drifting, either towards something or away from something. Not everyone, of course. But so many of these people, *especially* the people in the industry, have no idea how to steer their way through life. That's what made Dobro so special. He calmed them. He was a real comfort to them. And the best thing he did was that he didn't baby them. It's crazy. He worked for these people. They paid him. They paid him a lot. But his real value was that he was almost parental in the way he dealt with them. God, the stories I could tell."

Angelica and Dudley were sitting at the conference table in Dobro's office. She had grabbed up fish tacos from a street vendor, two for herself and four for Dudley.

"That's the way he was with my friend Delilah. Do you remember her?"

"God, yes," said Angelica. "Man, she could be demanding. The first time she called after I started here, it was like my second day on the job, I made the mistake of putting her on hold."

Dudley laughed at this, a tiny fleck of fish jettisoning from his wide mouth and back onto his plate.

"Sorry," he said. "Excuse me. How rude of me, but I know that she probably reacted in true Delilah fashion."

"After I put her through and she finishes her call with Dobro, he comes out to my desk and tells me to never put her on hold again. That if I do, she's going to leave the agency."

"That sounds about right," said Dudley. "Did you ever patch things up with her?"

"There was no patching. I was a peon employee to her. I mean, she wasn't rude or anything. I met her one time at a Christmas party Dobro threw. She never came to those things, but I think she was getting ready to leave the business…health issues…so she came to this one."

Dudley was smiling.

"Was she pleasant?"

"She wasn't anything, really. I walked up to her and introduced myself as Dobro's assistant and she told me it was nice to meet me and then she told me to go get her a glass of vodka."

"You have all kinds out here, don't you?" said Dudley.

Angelica nodded. She chewed a last bite of taco and swallowed before responding.

"Yes, we do. And their all in your flock now, Father Dudley."

He thought of this. His large and chubby right hand made its way to the thinning hair on his head. He wiped the corner of his mouth where crema from the tacos had settled with a paper napkin. He was so far out of his element, sitting at a table in Santa Monica, eating fish tacos, waiting for the next glistening client to seek his wisdom, that he had to marvel. Maybe this was God's work, he thought. Maybe something big could happen.

"I need to get some different clothes," he said to Angelica. "I didn't bring a lot of clothes with me. Well, I actually don't own a whole lot. And I only have one pair of shoes. These," he added, sliding a foot out from under the conference table.

"I can help with that. We can go shopping this afternoon if you're free. And you are free."

"That would be wonderful," he said. "I'm not much good at that sort of thing."

"Can I make a suggestion?" asked Angelica as she assembled the Styrofoam containers, paper napkins and plastic silverware, placing it all back into the large white bag it had arrived in.

"Of course," said Dudley.

"Can I suggest that you go heavy on black slacks and shirts? It has a real slimming effect, and it will play up the priest thing to your clients."

This made Dudley smile.

"And maybe go with an electric razor," she said.

Since going through late-age puberty, John Dudley had shaved every day of his life. Despite genuine effort, it was not uncommon for him to walk away from the bathroom mirror with patches his razor had missed. He also possessed a real knack for cutting himself.

"They're not my clients, but sure, that makes perfect sense. I always liked wearing black."

It was the following week, a Tuesday with perfect weather. Dudley parked Dobro's Mercedes in an open slot at the far end of the lot and trudged up the one flight of stairs to the office he now occupied. Although he made no effort to remember any of the appointments Angelica had scheduled for him, he recollected that he had one or two for the afternoon.

"Good morning," he said to Angelica as he passed her desk.

She handed him a piece of paper which contained handwritten notes for the meetings she had scheduled for him. One, an agent for a playwright trying to sell the most recent masterpiece to fly out of his client's supremely creative mind; the second, a young woman trying to make a splash in the world of stand-up comedy. She needed an agent and had been referred to The Dobro Temple Agency by an existing client.

"What does this mean?" he asked as he read the paper Angelica had handed him. "What does this mean? That she ends every performance by taking off all her clothes."

"That's what she does, John. I've not seen her, but apparently that's her hook to the audience. That's what she's known for. Full frontal nudity."

"But that's not funny," said Dudley. "That's very sad in a way."

211

"Tell her," said Angelica. "We have standards, right?"

Shortly before noon, John Dudley sat at Dobro's desk finishing a crossword puzzle. He was hungry and waited eagerly for Angelica to join him to discuss lunch. He always deferred to her preferences. Her selections were as close to exotic as he had eaten in a long while, and he truly was not a picky eater.

When Angelica appeared in the doorway, he sensed something had changed. She looked different, almost shaken, as if she were about to cry. Whatever this was, he hoped it would not delay lunch.

"What is it?" he asked. "You okay?"

She put her hands in front of her chest as if about to cup each breast. Dudley noticed the tears now trickling down her cheeks. A guttural, animal-like sound came from her throat as she made her first effort to talk.

Dudley rose and walked to her. He had helped people his entire life. Both during his time in the priesthood and afterwards, this overweight, unassuming man who so clearly lacked confidence of any kind, had been a surprising source of strength for everyone who seemed to need it. As he moved towards the doorway, he had no idea what to say or what to do. It would come to him.

He placed a hand on Angelica's shoulder. She was beginning to regain control of her breathing and held up her hand in an indication that an answer was forthcoming. She took a deep breath and looked directly and intensely into Dudley's eyes.

"There's a man on the phone," she said. "He's a police officer at some Indian reservation in Idaho somewhere."

She swallowed with difficulty. The world, for an instant, stopped spinning. Dudley could hear dust settling on the floor beneath his feet.

"They found Sara's car."

Paul Danko parked his metallic blue Porsche in the slot reserved for Dobro Temple. He had no time to waste looking for a parking place. He bounded up the stairs to the second floor three at a time. He did not wait for Angelica to wave him through to Dobro's office. He entered and she followed.

"Talk to me," he said to no one in particular.

"Angelica?" said Dudley as he motioned to where she stood in the doorway.

"This cop from Idaho, some Indian reservation cop, he calls and says they've located Sara's car. They ran the license number, and it came up. So, he looks us up and figures he'd let us know where it was."

"How did they…" asked Dudley.

"The car's registered to the agency," Danko interrupted. "The agency owns the car. That's how he knew to call us." Then to Angelica: "where in Idaho?"

"I don't know," she said. "Somewhere where they have Indians."

"You got a name and a number?"

"Let me get it," she said as she hurried out of the room.

"What should we do, Paul?" asked Dudley.

"I'm going to call the guy and find out where he is. Then I'm going to go to the airport."

Paul Danko sat at Dobro's desk and made notes on a yellow legal pad as he spoke. The police officer, a member of the Poshone Tribe located in east-central Idaho had been asked to run a plate number for a colleague.

"May I ask who the colleague was?" said Danko.

"It was our doctor here on the rez," said the officer. "Her name's Jillian Andrews. Doctor Jillian Andrews."

"Can I get a number please?" asked Paul. "We're dealing with a missing person case. It might be very helpful for me to speak to her."

Thirty-five agonizing minutes later Angelica patched through a call from Doctor Andrews. Paul put the call on speaker.

"Thank you so much for getting back to me so quickly," said Danko. "We're dealing with a missing person case here. We're trying to locate a young woman named Sara Temple. She's been unaccounted for for about eighteen months. That's her car. The one you passed along to the Tribal Officer."

"Well, I don't know anyone by that name, Mr. Danko, but we did have a young woman present at our clinic in Dark Mountain who had been...allegedly now...held somewhat against her will. But her name is Mandy Mist. I've not heard the name Sara Temple. I can't say as how these things are related, but they might be."

"Any information you can give me on the other girl, this Mandy girl, might be of great help," said Paul.

"The person you really want to talk to is one of our nurses. Her name's Rebecca Moon, and she works at the clinic in Dark Mountain. She actually visited the place where this Mandy Mist was living. She knows a lot more about this than I do."

"I hate to impose," said Danko, "but might you have a number where she can be reached?"

"Sure," said Jillian. "You can reach her at the clinic. I'm pretty sure she's on days right now. You may be able to talk to her right now."

"Thanks very much, Doctor. You've been a big help."

He hung the phone up and looked immediately to Angelica.

"Two things, doll," he said.

Years ago, this would have been a common form of address from Paul. But she had not heard it in eons. She had certainly grown into a more mature woman, less *doll-like* for sure. But there was something else. She sensed it and it made her smile. Danko was invigorated. He had picked up a scent he thought forever to be lost. He youthened as he sat pointing at her.

"Call this Rebecca woman and tell her what the deal is. You don't need to be careful with any of it. The more she knows, the more help she might be able to help us. And tell her that I'm on my way to the airport and that I'll be there as soon as I can."

"What's the second thing?" asked Angelica.

"Get me a flight to the closest airport you can find to Dark Mountain. Wherever the hell that is. And I'll need a car when I land."

"Got it," she said.

Dudley had been standing silently out of the way. This was adventure and he had lived his life removed from adventure. He wanted greatly for Sara to be found, but his desire for this paled in comparison to what he assumed Paul Danko and Angelica were experiencing. He stood on the periphery and drank all of this in.

"I want to go with you," he heard himself saying to Danko. "I made the same promise to Dobro as you did, and I want to be there. I won't get in the way. I promise."

Danko took a cursory look at Dudley. Out-of-shape, aging, soft and probably no damn good in a fight, if that's what it came to. But there was something about the former priest. Danko knew that Dudley was eager to avoid any and all conflict, that he would waffle at the first sign of trouble. But he also saw a depth of character that seemed to be just under the surface. He knew that Dobro Temple was the most gifted person he'd ever known at reading people. And Dobro had wanted the priest here. That had to mean something.

"Make it two tickets," he said to Angelica.

Dudley tried to smile but was already thinking of the flurry of events the next several hours of his life were certain to become.

"I don't have clean clothes," he said. "I don't have a change of clothes or a toothbrush or anything."

"You're not going to need any of that," said Danko. "Let's go."

As Paul walked past Angelica, he paused and kissed her lightly on the cheek.

"Wish us luck, doll."

At the airport as they waited to board their flight to Boise, Paul and Dudley bought new shirts, underwear and socks at a high-end store catering to men who wished themselves membership in the high classes. John selected a black turtle-neck but replaced it with a standard button-down dress shirt after trying it on. The cut of the neck-line made it appear as if his head was resting directly on top of his chest. It also reminded him of the collars he had worn while in the priesthood. For the most part, those were not memories he wished to relive.

"Much better," said Danko after his traveling companion had swapped shirts.

"I've never owned a shirt that cost this much," said Dudley after Paul had paid for their selections with a company credit card.

They bought small travel kits containing a toothbrush, toothpaste and mouthwash at the newsstand next to their gate and placed them in the large shopping bag their clothing was in. One item of luggage between them which Dudley carried as they boarded.

The two men spoke very little on the flight out. When Dudley asked what kind of plan of action Paul Danko was considering upon their arrival, the response was clipped.

"I won't know until I know more," said Danko. "I'll call Angelica as soon as we land to see what the situation is. Hopefully, she'll have been able to reach this nurse we want to talk to. We'll play it by ear."

Dudley sat in his first-class seat and sipped coffee. He watched Paul sit without movement, his eyes closed, his breathing measured. He knew that Danko was not sleeping, that he was calculating. This observation filled him with confidence but did not alleviate his trepidation.

Angelica had reserved a luxury sedan, and Danko sent John Dudley to find it and drive it around to the loading area of the airport while he called the office for new information. After becoming somewhat accustomed to driving from Topanga into Santa Monica and back for several weeks, John was certain that negotiating traffic in Idaho would be a breeze. He hoped that Danko would let him drive.

"Want me to drive?" he asked from behind the wheel as Danko appeared from inside the terminal.

"No," said Paul. "We're in a hurry."

Danko handed Dudley his notebook.

"Angelica gave me directions. They're on the last page. You're the navigator. We're going to the clinic in a place called Dark Mountain."

It was late afternoon pushing into evening as they left the Interstate and headed deeper into the mountains on the two-lane road that would take them to Dark Mountain. Dudley realized that he had not had lunch, that he had not eaten a thing since the English Muffin he had toasted that morning in Dobro's kitchen.

As they drove away from population there was precious little in the way of food. Gas station hotdogs, bags of chips, chocolate bars.

"Did you eat lunch at all?" he asked Danko.

"I didn't. Let's get to where we're going and see what the plan is."

Dudley added hunger to the assemblage of disconcerting sensations he was experiencing.

"There it is," said John Dudley as the approached the clinic two and one half hours later. "There it is on the left."

Danko turned the sedan into the lot and parked in one of slots reserved for visitors.

"Let's go," he said as he quickly got out of the car and walked with long strides to the main entrance.

John Dudley had a hard time keeping up.

The young man sitting at the front desk just inside the waiting area was pleasant and went off to get Rebecca Moon immediately upon Danko's request. Very clearly, he had anticipated their arrival.

She followed the young man into the waiting area and walked with purpose to where Danko and John Dudley were standing. She extended her hand first to Danko and then to John.

"I'm Rebecca Moon," she said. "A woman who works with you, Angelica, called me and told me you were on your way. She told me about the girl you're looking for...Sara Temple. I'm not sure I know anything about her specifically, but I'll do anything I can to help you."

"Is there some place we can talk a bit more privately?" asked Danko.

"I'm sorry, but not really," said Rebecca. "There's very limited office space here. Maybe we could just sit over there by the window."

The three of them took seats lined along the window, their backs to the parking lot. Rebecca sat in the middle and directed most of her attention to Danko on her right.

She told him everything. She told him about Mandy, about the marks on her neck from being locked in an iron collar. She told him about Jeff Mist and his belief in polygamy, his contention that he was the voice of God, his zealotry. She told him about Mist following her and about the mutilated bird she had found on her porch. About the trip she and Winton Crow had made to the Mist farm. And finally, about the car.

"Thank God Winton remembered the license plate. And thank God Doctor Andrews knew those people at the tribal police to be able to find you. I hope and pray that the girl you're looking for can be found. I didn't see anyone out there except this Jeff guy, but Mandy told us that there were other wives there. I hope this helps you. The local police… these deputies…they seemed less than interested in pursuing this any further."

"In all likelihood we won't be needing their assistance," said Paul.

"Can you give us directions to the farm, Nurse Moon?"

"Rebecca. Please. Sure, I can. Do you have something to write on?"

After neatly writing the directions to the Mist farm in his notepad, Danko rose to leave.

"One last thing," he said, "was that motel and the bar back in town, were those our only options for tonight? We'll probably visit Mr. Mist in the morning, and we'll need a place to spend the night and get a bite to eat."

"Yes. Those are your only options. But they're not bad. I stayed in that motel when I first got here. And I've eaten in that pub quite a few times."

"I don't know your schedule," said Danko, "but we would love to buy you dinner if you're free later."

She smiled at this.

"That would be nice, but I won't get out of here until almost nine tonight. You guys are probably hungry and tired from your trip."

"We are," said John Dudley. "We really are."

She walked with them the few steps to the main door and again shook each man's hand.

"Could I ask you to let me know if you find anything useful about the girl you're looking for?" she said. "I've felt bad that I know there might be other women out there who are being mistreated, and that I can't seem to get anyone to do anything about it. I would really like to know what you find."

"I give you my word," said Danko. "Someone will call you before we leave the state of Idaho."

"Thanks," she said.

"I can't thank you enough," said Danko.

As the two men drove back towards town and the motel, Dudley was glad that the nurse had turned down the invitation to dinner. He was famished and hoped that the motel lobby had a vending machine.

Despite the long day Dudley did not sleep with any sense of comfort. His night was a series of interrupted cat naps, and he finally gave up just after four, showered and dressed. He liked the way his new shirt fit him. Angelica was right: black was his color.

He met Paul Danko in the lobby at six sharp. Nothing in town was open, so they drank colas from the vending machine as they drove towards the Mist farm.

"It goes without saying that I'll do the talking, right?" said Danko as they pulled off the main road and headed back into the mountain where Mist lived.

Dudley nodded. He heart was in his throat. He recalled the nurse telling them that she and an old Indian fellow had made this same trip, and he marveled at her courage. He had

Danko, the right guy for just about any touchy situation; she had had the old Indian.

The sun was just making its way above the tree line when Danko eased the sedan into Mist's driveway. The shabby house looked empty; its windows were dark.

Dudley almost peed himself when Paul Danko leaned on the horn. He heard a dog bark from somewhere. He surprised himself by getting out of the car before Danko. When Paul stepped around to his side of the car, he was relieved.

The door opened slowly, and Mist stepped out on to the sagging porch. Dudley was immediately calmed. This man wearing pajama bottoms and an old sweater, standing twenty yards away from them in his bare feet, was not daunting at all. Not even to John Dudley.

Paul Danko was a large man, powerfully built. He was smooth and sophisticated, he dressed impeccably. But he was a man who had attained a comfortable position in life not by talking, but by taking the actions necessary to accomplish what he needed done. For a moment, Dudley felt sorry for Mist. He was thin and dirty and clearly over his head where Danko was concerned.

"What can I do for you?" he asked from the porch.

"We're looking for the daughter of a friend of ours," said Danko. "Sara Temple. You ever heard of her?"

Mist was silent. He glanced quickly at Sara's car parked almost in the bushes off to the side of the house.

"Yeah," said Danko smiling. "That's her car. Actually, it's not her car. It's owned by her father, so it could be considered stolen if I wanted to get the authorities involved in this. But I don't."

"Again, what can I do for you," said Mist, recovered slightly from the sudden surprise of the visit.

"I'd like to see Sara if she's here. I'd like to speak to her and make sure she's alright."

The silence that transpired just then was heavy as dusty air. It portended a situation that most assuredly would be resolved only by quick thinking and, perhaps, violence. Dudley silently thanked his own private God that Danko was standing beside him.

"She's my wife," said Mist. "God has placed her here with me so that I can take care of her, provide for her, mentor her as she grows…"

"That's all well and good," said Danko interrupting, "but I would really like to say hello to her. If you let me do that, just say hello and ask her a question or two, we'll get out of here and let you get on with your day."

"What if I feel it best for her not to see you? As her husband."

"That would put a whole new spin on our visit here," said Danko. "Let's not go to that place right now. Why don't you just ask her to come out and say hi to me?"

Mist raised a finger asking for a moment. He stepped back into the darkened house. Dudley felt his heartbeat quicken in his chest.

"Go stand around the other side of the car," said Danko.

"I'm good," said John Dudley.

It was the singularly most courageous action of his life.

Danko had not seen Sara in almost two years. But this was Dobro's daughter emerging from the house and standing next to Mist. She was rail thin, and her hair was longer, but this was Sara. He was certain.

"Hello, Sara. Do you remember me? Paul Danko. I worked with your father. Do you remember me?"

The young woman nodded. Her expression showed no emotion. Her eyes were glassy, and she seemed incapable of looking directly at anything for more than a few seconds.

"Are you doing alright?" asked Danko. "Is there anything I can do for you? Do you need any help with anything? Anything at all?"

"Tell this man that you're fine, Sara," said Mist. "Tell him that you're my wife and that your place is here with me."

Danko took two steps towards the porch. He wanted a closer look, but more importantly wanted Sara to see him more clearly.

"I'm fine," she whispered. "I'm really fine, Mr. Danko. I like living here with my husband. I'm doing well, really, I am."

Danko's recollection of Sara was that of a head-strong and free-spirited girl who grew into a confident and polished young woman. This was not Sara he was talking to. Some part of her had been removed. Her shoulders were not squared, her spine was not straight.

"You don't look fine," said Danko. "You look like you might need to see a doctor. Why don't you let us drive you back to town and get you looked at by a nurse we know? Your husband can come along. It'll give us a chance to catch up. And we'll bring you right back."

"We're not going anywhere," said Mist. "Sara, tell this man that we're not going anywhere with him."

"We're not going anywhere with you," she said in voice softer than a raindrop. "No offense, but I want to stay here with my husband. I don't want to go with you."

Danko stood silently. He ran his hand through his short hair and kicked gently at a stone that was in the driveway at his feet.

"Fair enough," he said. "Sara, it was great seeing you, doll. We miss you. All of us miss you."

Danko looked directly at Mist while continuing to speak to Sara.

"And we'll be back tomorrow just to say hello again, and to make sure there isn't something we can do to help you."

"I told you she's not going anywhere," said Mist as Danko and Dudley stepped back to the car.

Danko spun quickly around and took three steps back towards the porch. Mist leaned back towards the porch door.

"Save it," said Danko.

And then with a smile, "save it until tomorrow."

Dudley was dying to ask Paul Danko what their next step might be as they drove back towards town and their motel. But he knew that Danko was running a bit hot after his confrontation with Jeff Mist and made the prudent decision to wait.

Neither man spoke until they were sitting in a booth ordering breakfast back in Dark Mountain.

"Can we call the cops?" asked Dudley. "It seemed rather obvious to me that that woman was being controlled. And from what the nurse told us, there's got to be some sort of criminal activity going on out there, right?"

"They're not going to be of any help," said Paul, "or they would have intervened already. Just let me think."

"Do you think we could just take her?" asked Dudley. "I mean, couldn't we just take her back for her own good?"

Danko shook his head.

"She an adult: She has told us that she's fine and that she wants to stay with her husband. And it doesn't matter if he's really her husband or not. If we just march in there and pull her out, we could get charged with kidnapping. And that would do her no good at all. Just let me think," he said. "Just give me a little time to come up with something."

The men sat for the remainder of their breakfast in silence. Frustration hung in the air like smoke from a dirty chimney. Danko paid the bill and the two men headed back to the motel. Halfway across the street Dudley stopped Paul Danko, pulling his shoulder back. The former priest was smiling.

"I have an idea," he said without releasing Danko from his rather weak grip. "I have an idea."

At a few minutes before noon the following day, Paul Danko turned the rental car on to the side road leading to the Mist place. The two men had risen early and had enjoyed a nice breakfast at The Pub, but John Dudley was now hungry for his lunch. He was glad he'd come along on this trip. He took very seriously the commitment he had made to Sara's father, that he would do his best to find her and to make certain that she was safe. He also took his meals very seriously and would be glad when this adventure was concluded, and he was back on a more regular schedule.

They were visiting later in the day than they had the previous morning. The sky had cleared, and the sun was fully up. The brighter exposure didn't help the appearance of Mist's house. Like sunshine on the wrinkles of an old person's face, the place looked shabbier and in a greater state of disrepair.

Danko pulled the car to a stop and stepped out. Dudley waited this time for his partner to come around to his side of the car before opening his door and climbing out. They had discussed the fact that Mist might own a firearm…they suspected that most of the people living in these mountains probably did…and this was the first time that Dudley truly experienced the fear of being shot.

The door opened slightly and then closed again. The two men waited in the driveway.

Mist came out of the house dressed exactly as he had been the previous day. He assumed the same posture in exactly the same spot on his porch. He wore no shoes.

"I thought I made myself clear yesterday," he said, "I thought both Sara and I made ourselves clear yesterday. Her place is with me. She's not going anywhere. Now I'm going to have to ask you to get off my property."

"Here's the thing, Mr. Mist," said Danko. "We started thinking about this predicament here and we have one more question to ask Sara. Just one. If you'll let us see her for thirty seconds and ask her just one more thing, I give you my word, we'll leave, and you won't see us again."

Mist took a moment to think about this. Dudley thought he saw movement in one of the windows looking out on to the porch. He wondered if Paul had detected it.

"You give me your word?" said Mist.

"Yes, sir. I do," said Danko.

Mist turned and opened the door to the house. He said something that neither Dudley nor Paul Danko could decipher. Seconds later, Sara emerged dressed in the same clothing as she had worn the day before.

"Good morning, Sara," said Paul Danko. "I hope you're doing alright this morning."

"Let's get on with it," said Mist. "You said one question, then you would leave. Let's have the question."

"Fair enough," said Danko.

He motioned to Dudley standing beside him. At his cue, John Dudley turned to the car and opened the rear door. The woman who stepped out of the car was tall and trim. She had black hair and possessed a certain calm that no one else standing there in the sunlight that morning owned.

"Hi, Sara. Remember me?" asked Pei Ling.

Danko had not watched Pei Ling step out of the car. Nor had he looked at Mist as this was transpiring. His gaze was directed solely at Sara. He wanted to see her reaction. He wanted to see if a spark appeared.

What he saw, truly for the first time, was fear. He surmised accurately that Pei Ling's presence had allowed Sara to contemplate, just for an instant, being home and away from this place. And the comfort that this thought had given her was immediately pushed away by the fear that it might not happen. That she could not reach that place because of the man standing beside her.

Pei Ling took several steps towards the porch. Jeff Mist placed his hand on Sara's shoulder.

"Do you know her?" he asked.

There are moments, at the end, when an animal so near death rises up one last time to confront the reality that life is to be ended. From some deep and unknown place, the strength and courage and belief are summoned for one last cry into the pending darkness. This was such a moment for Sara Temple.

As if in slow motion, she brushed Mist's hand from her shoulder and stepped towards the driveway. She met Pei Ling at the bottom of the sagging steps. The embrace was pure and contained every emotion in the human experience. Sara cried and Pei Ling held her more closely than she had in all the years they had been together.

"Sara, you need to come back in the house," said Mist.

At this, Pei Ling looked at the man standing on the porch. She did this without releasing Sara.

"She wants to come home with me," said Pei Ling. "Don't you, Sara?"

"She wants to get back in the house and honor her God and her husband," said Mist. "Isn't that right, Sara?"

Without turning back to the porch and still fully absorbed in Pei Ling's embrace, Sara whispered.

"I want to go home," she said.

To Mist, this remark was a signal that his control over this young woman, while still strong, had dissipated. To Pei Ling, it meant that Sara was reachable. That it would take time and many, many hours of counseling, but that the Sara she had known was there somewhere in the shadows and could be returned to the light. For Paul Danko, this meant that it was the moment for swift and decisive action. It was an opening. It was a flinch in the stalemate that he would not allow to pass. And to John Dudley, it was magic. His heart was filled as he thought of his friend Dobro. That Dobro could now rest in peace.

Danko stepped to the bottom of the porch and ushered the two women to the car, not taking his eyes off Mist. When Sara and Pei Ling were safely in the back seat, he closed the door.

"Get in the car," he said to John Dudley.

Danko walked back towards the porch and stopped just short of the bottom step.

"Keep the car," he said to Mist. "You're not going to see any of us again. It's yours."

"My wife needs to be here with me," said Mist. Despite his attempt at bravado, he looked small and filled with doubt. His words were stale and dry.

"That may be," said Danko, "but I made a promise to someone to bring this girl home and I intend to keep that promise."

Danko turned and stepped toward the car. Mist was silent. He did not move.

"One more thing," said Danko as he turned back towards the porch. "If I ever see you again, anywhere, I'm going to assume that you're there to cause harm to someone I know, and I'm going to end your life. I don't make threats, Mr. Mist. I perform acts of duty. And ending your life would be an act of duty. Nothing more."

Danko remained facing Mist, staring at the man in the drab, ill-fitting sweater. Mist looked down.

"You'll burn in hell for what you've done," said Mist in a voice that could almost not be heard.

Danko smiled.

"Buddy, you have no idea how true that statement is," he said.

They drove without stopping to the airport in Boise. With the exception of the few moments it took as she passed through the metal detector and once, for ninety seconds when she used the bathroom, Sara did not release Pei Ling's hand from her own.

CHAPTER FOUR

Howard Straz sat at his desk in his small office at the clinic. His door was open as it almost always was. He was pouring over the previous month's profit and loss statement. He was pleased that snow removal had come in under budget, but was a bit concerned that reimbursements from the state were lagging.

Rebecca knocked gently on the wall outside.

"Nurse Moon," he said with a touch of excitement in his voice.

"Am I disturbing you?" she asked.

"Yes, you are. Thank you for doing so. A necessary evil, but these reports make my hair hurt. Please, come in."

She entered and took a seat across the desk in one of the two, ages-old metal chairs that were for visitors. She would have guessed that they should have been replaced a decade ago, but she would not have put it past Straz to have kept them as a tactic to keep visits to his office short and to the point. It would have been near impossible for anyone sitting any length of time to retain feeling in the bottom half of his or her body.

"I think you should know that I just got off the phone with one of those men who visited me the other evening. The ones about the missing girl."

He looked fully up from the computer screen resting at an angle at the side of his desk.

"What did they find? I've actually been praying about that."

"Your prayers apparently worked, Howard. He called from the airport in Boise. They're on their way home. She was out there at that guy's farm. Almost a year and a half I think he said. Anyway, she's safe and sound. Well, probably not too sound. Heaven knows what she's been through."

Howard Straz closed his eyes. He devoutly nodded his head. It was meditation without the humming.

"You've saved a girl's life, Rebecca. I don't know if I've ever witnessed, at least personally, courage like you displayed. Who takes it upon themselves to go out to that place and face down that man? Quite impressive."

"I never would have done it if he hadn't threatened me with that whole dead bird thing. That girl from Los Angeles would still be out there wearing that iron collar if this guy hadn't put that on my porch. And I never would have gone out there if it hadn't been for my friend Winton. He really gave me the courage to go out there. I'm bringing him to the next employee party, by the way."

She paused for a moment as she recalled her trip to the Mist farm.

"Oh," she said, "the girl told the guy, the girl who had been out there, the girl from LA, that the only woman left out at that place was this Mist guy's sister or something. So, he had two wives and a sister out there, and apparently a brother off and on. How twisted is all of that?"

"It's beyond comprehension," said Straz. "It makes you wonder what goes on behind closed doors, doesn't it?"

"I'm not going to drive around wondering that for a while," said Rebecca. "I've had my dose of adventure for quite a while, thank you very much."

Straz smiled.

"Back to the employee party, that would be the Summer picnic," he said. "It's a lot of fun. More kid oriented. Games, contests, real Americana. My kids love it. I do all the grilling."

Straz paused for effect.

"Does this mean I might be able to talk you into another six months with us? You've settled in so fast, and you're so good at what you do. I've seen the other nurses on staff pay attention to you. We'd love to keep you for a while. And if there's anything I can do to convince you, are you alright with your shifts? The cabin working out for you?"

"The cabin's fine," she said. "And I have my little Indian man out there. He and I have actually kind of become friends. We're drinking buddies, I think. But I need to ask you something before I answer your question."

"Anything," said Howard Straz.

Rebecca inhaled deeply and exhaled slowly just as she often coached pregnant women in labor to do as a means to mitigate pain.

"Has anyone from the agency contacted you about my being here? I mean, *is she still there, how's she doing* kind of stuff?"

"Not word one," he said. "Why is it you ask?"

Again, she paused for a breathing exercise.

"I'm going to tell you something that I probably shouldn't, but I need to if I'm going to stay on here. This place has grown on me a little. Like I said, I have my little Indian man, I love Wanda Ripple, I can tolerate Pocker. Jillian is one of the best doctors I've ever been around."

Straz did not speak as she took several seconds to regain momentum.

"Did you ever wonder why I've moved around so much? To so many out-of-the-way places?"

"I simply thought it was a lifestyle choice on your part. That you didn't want anything to do with the big city. And that you had a bad case of wanderlust or something like that."

"I'm going to tell you something and I will completely understand if you want me to leave immediately after hearing it. I love being a nurse. It's all I ever really wanted to do. Even as a little girl…well, all little girls probably go through a stage like that, taking care of their dolls and all of that. But I never outgrew it. It fulfills me if that makes sense?"

"It does. And it shows in your work," said Straz.

"I helped two people end their own lives. Almost five years ago. In Pennsylvania. They were so old, and he was probably weeks away from dying. And she simply didn't want to go on without him. I was doing a home nursing thing, working with a hospice group. They just got to me. And when they brought the subject up…well, she brought it up first…I thought about it and decided to help them."

"There are states where that type of thing is allowed," said Straz.

"This wasn't one of them. I was questioned by the police. I mean, it was odd that they died at the same time. The same afternoon. It was in the Fall of the year. They kind of wrote it down that the guy died, and that his wife overdosed on the drug he was on right after that. They asked me if I had supplied any extra dosage of the drug. I lied and told them that I hadn't."

Howard Straz sat motionless and let the moment rest in the ether between himself and Rebecca Moon. He knew now that she had committed a crime. A questionable crime, to be sure, and one whose legitimacy could be debated for hours.

"And this is why you began to travel? All the remote locations," he said.

"Now you know my secret," she said. "In case anyone was looking for me, I wanted to stay a step ahead of them. I'll stay if you can keep it to yourself and if you still want me."

"Nurse Moon, you just rescued a girl from hell. I only have one question for you."

"Yeah, and what's that?" she asked.

"Do you prefer hotdogs or hamburgers?"

Sara Temple spoke when spoken to and not more than that. She contributed nothing to conversations that took place among Pei Ling, Danko and John Dudley. She offered up no thoughts or opinions. She answered questions, but only in short sentences and with a timid voice, as if speaking with a sore throat.

She sat in the window seat on the flight back to Los Angeles, Pei Ling beside her. The two women held hands. They sipped at the drinks resting on their tray tables with their free hands as if their other wrists were handcuffed together. Sara cried until she had no more tears, and then she cried some more.

"I'm not going to talk you to death," whispered Pei Ling. "I know you need some time to process things. You need lots of time. But you have that now, Sara. All of us love you. All of us are going to be there for you."

Sara did not respond. She continued to hold Pei Ling's hand as she looked out the window to the patchwork quilt of farmland below.

"I need to tell you something about your father," said Pei Ling in a very quiet voice.

"Is my father angry at me?" asked Sara.

Pei Ling paused before answering. She had given a great deal of thought as to when Sara should be given this news. She decided to allow the moment to come to her. She'd know it when she sensed it, and she sensed that it was now.

"Your father passed away a short time ago," she said. "He was sick. He was very sick. It happened pretty quickly. But he was not angry. He worried, of course. But he loved you unconditionally. He told me that. And he asked me to tell you that in the event I ever saw you again."

Sara looked at Pei Ling. Her eyes were red and swollen, the blue more pronounced. The brown of Pei Ling's eyes didn't look away. The two women remained focused on each other. Something passed between them just then that neither could recognize or label. It was some essence of understanding that did not need to be named, only experienced. Pei Ling wondered how much more emotion one person could handle in a day; Sara felt love for the first time in many, many months.

As they waited for valets to bring Pei Ling's and Paul Danko's cars to them, they discussed logistics. Pei Ling took Sara's hand and steered her away from the two men.

"You can stay wherever you want tonight," she said. "I'm going to make an appointment for you to be seen by one of my colleagues in the morning. Don't worry, it's a woman. I work with her, and she's very nice. But tonight, you can stay with me at my place, or you can stay with Father Dudley at home. He's been living there since just before your father passed away. I've gotten to know him quite well. He's a very nice man, Sara. I'm sorry, I can't stay at the house with you. I have too early a morning. But you'll be comfortable with him if that's what you want to do."

The cars arrived and Danko gave five dollar bills to each of the valets.

"What's the plan?" he asked Pei Ling.

Pei Ling looked back as Sara.

"Sara?" she asked.

"I think I want to go home," she said.

Pei Ling drove Dudley and Sara back to the Agency to pick up the Mercedes. She stepped out from behind the wheel and stood facing Sara as the young woman was walking from car to car.

"Remember how strong you are," she whispered. "You may not feel very strong right now, but you are. Your father made you this way."

"I'm exhausted," said Sara.

"Get some sleep tonight," said Pei Ling. "I'll call the house tomorrow and give the details of your appointment to John."

Dudley drove the car along the ocean and then up into Topanga. Sara did not speak and the quietness the expensive sedan provided made Dudley feel like he was in a confessional booth waiting for the next sinner to creep in.

It was fully dark when Sara and Dudley climbed the steps to the deck of the house. She turned the pool lights on as she passed the switch located just outside the sliding glass doors to the house. The ethereal glow from the light blue sides of the pool seemed to provide her with a sense of comfort.

Dudley went into the house. He was not certain what dinner options might be available, but he was rather instantly aware that he had eaten very little over the past many hours. Sara entered the house as might a burglar, unsure of where furniture might be placed, cautious in her movements.

"Are you sleeping in my dad's room?" she asked.

Dudley was standing at a cupboard in the kitchen inspecting cans of food.

"Yes," he said, "but he told me to. He told me that it was alright to do that."

"I'm just asking because I want to go in there for a few minutes. I need to go in there to get my bearings, and I don't want to intrude on your privacy."

John placed a can of soup on the counter and went to the door of the bedroom he had been using. He opened the door and stood back to allow Sara a wide berth. He watched her enter her father's bedroom. She moved to Dobro's desk and sat in his chair. She picked up a glass paperweight, a gift from some client, and inspected it. She opened the drawer in the center of the desk and removed a letter opener, a tiny stapler, an expensive Mont Blanc pen that her father had used to make notes as he spoke to clients on the phone. As she walked back towards the door, she allowed her hand to trail along the edge of the bed. John Dudley felt it intrusive to watch all of this, but he could not look away. Sara silently wept the entire time.

"I'll heat up some soup if you're hungry," he said as she passed through the kitchen on her way to her bedroom.

"Okay. Thank you," she said without turning back to him.

"Any preference on what kind of soup?" he asked.

She shook her head as she entered her room and closed the door behind her.

They ate clam chowder and crackers with large glasses of water as they sat diagonally from each other at the dining area table. Dudley was in the chair at the head of the table; Sara sat in what the priest presumed was her old spot at his side.

"I'm sorry that I'm not much of a cook," he said.

"It's alright. I was hungry," she whispered.

"My wife...well, we never really got married...but the woman with whom I had a child, she was a terrific cook. She owned a very nice restaurant before I met her. Gosh, she could cook about anything."

"Where is she?" asked Sara.

"She and my daughter Claudia live in Miami. She... Nuncia...married some businessman type and they live in

Miami. I go visit every other year or so. Claudia's a little older than you. She works for Caesar. That's Nuncia's husband. Caesar Salada. She's a very nice young woman."

"I'm sure she is," said Sara. "I don't know what to call you," she added. "I've heard Dudley, Father Dudley, John. Which do I use?"

Dudley smiled. The question did not amuse him; the fact that he truly was uncertain as to how he should answer it did.

"Call me whatever you'd like," he said. "I'm not a practicing priest any longer, but so many people seem to forget that. I met with a couple of your father's clients last week…that's a story all to itself, believe me…but they seemed so delighted to call me Father. So, call me what you'd like."

"I'll just go with John," she said. "That's what my dad called you. He talked about you quite often. He admired your commitment to helping people. Especially that singer Delilah Duncan. He said you comforted her."

He watched as she dipped a small piece of cracker into her soup. Her hands were so delicate, her fingertips capable of such gentleness that it made him instantly sad. He wondered how anyone could harm such a person as this.

"Can I ask you something, John?" she said.

He looked up from his own bowl to her eyes.

"What happened to your wrists?" she said. "That might be rude to ask, but I have to know."

He breathed deeply in and out and shifted in his chair. It sounded like a large dog settling into his bed of straw for the night.

"I tried to kill myself. Many years ago. That's how I came to know your father. I was in a hospital of sorts that one of his clients, Delilah, was also in. That's how I came to know him. To become friends with him."

These were memories that did not often surface in John Dudley's life. They were not painful as much as they bordered on melancholy. They made him think of his daughter and of the relationships with many others which he now missed.

"I'm sorry. I probably shouldn't have asked that," said Sara.

There were several moments of silence.

"I thought of it," she finally said. "It could be so horrible when he got mad. Or when his brother was around. Mandy and I…that's the girl who got away…we talked about doing it all the time. I don't really know why we didn't. I think we just got used to suffering."

"I can't answer that," said Dudley. "It's such a private and personal thing. No two times ever sync, you know? No two motivations or rationales are the same. At least that's what I think."

"Why did you?" asked Sara.

The priest looked directly at her. This was not comfortable conversation, but it was needed and necessary, and he knew this. He had entertained the notion, slight as it was, that he might be able to help Sara; that his support, his listening, his counseling background just might enable him to get her somewhat back to who she was before. But before any of that was possible, she needed to trust him. He needed to open himself to her. He needed to answer the question.

"There was a little boy. A long time ago. Something bad was happening to him, and I failed to act in a way to help him. I rationalized my lack of not doing anything. I hid behind the black clothes. I hid behind the church and kept quiet. That's my cross to bear," he said.

"What happened to the little boy?" she asked.

"He killed himself in his parents' garage," said Dudley.

"I'm sorry I asked all those questions," said Sara. "But if we're going to be living here together, I just wanted to know."

"I don't have to live here," said John. "I don't know how you want to proceed with all of this, but I can go back to Virginia if you would like me to. I came out here to be with your father and he asked if I would stay a while. But if you would like the house to yourself, I will completely understand.""

She stood from the table and carried her bowl and empty glass to the kitchen.

"I don't want to be alone right now," she said. "And who's safer to be with than a priest, right?"

He hoisted himself up from the table.

"Leave your dishes," he said. "I'll load the dishwasher."

"I'm going to bed," said Sara.

"Listen," he said, "if you need anything at all, even if it's in the middle of the night, wake me. Just holler, okay? I'll leave my door open so that I'll hear you. Even if you just want to talk, okay?"

She nodded. Never do we anticipate nightmares, but the probability of a restless night's sleep was strong, and John Dudley knew this.

"John," she said just before entering her room. "Could you take me shopping tomorrow for some clothes? I really don't have anything to wear."

When she had gone into her room and closed the door, and when John Dudley had rinsed their soup bowls and placed them in the dishwasher, he turned off the overhead light in the kitchen and stood in the semi-darkness.

He thought back to his days in the church. He had not been a very good priest and he knew this. He had accepted his limitations to ever be a strong and nurturing father to his daughter, and he had passed that responsibility over to a man he did not really know.

But he had helped people in his life, and he knew this also. The call-in radio show that he had hosted at the direction of the indominable Delilah Duncan, the counseling sessions through his volunteer work at a small rehabilitation clinic back in Virginia, and now, quite possibly, this damaged young woman rescued from such a dark and horrifying place. He didn't know much, but he knew that he was capable of listening with the best of them. And he knew when signs appeared, how to interpret them and how to respond to them. And Sara had used the word *tomorrow*. It was a task on the schedule. It was something she needed or wanted to do.

This was a sign, and John Dudley knew it was. He went to the sliding glass door and locked it before walking quietly into Dobro's bedroom. He closed the door before changing into pajamas, and then opened it before climbing into bed. It had been a long, grinding day filled with more thought and emotion than he had probably ever experienced. If he dreamed that night, he did not remember when he woke in the morning.

She found a pair of jeans and a sweatshirt in her closet the next morning. Never a large person, always fit and trim from swimming, the weight she had lost was noticeable. Her clothes hung on her as would a larger woman's serape.

John was making a breakfast of sausage patties and scrambled eggs when she emerged from her room, two frying pans in action on the stove top. He wore black slacks and a black button-down shirt and was doing his best not to scorch the eggs.

"Good morning," he said. "I was just about to come in and get you. Pei Ling called, and your appointment is at eleven. I thought we could do that and then get some lunch before we shop for some clothes for you."

Sara stepped to the island counter in bare feet. She sat on a stool and watched Dudley inexpertly stir the eggs.

"Did you put some butter in the pan?" she asked.

He looked at her with a trace of panic in his eyes.

"If you put butter in first, the eggs won't stick to the pan while you're cooking them," she said.

Dudley removed the pan from the stove. The eggs were black at the edges and the smell of smoke began to creep into the air in the kitchen.

"John, put the pan in the sink…the side with the disposal…and run some cold water in it. We can clean it up later."

He followed Sara's directions and returned to his post at the stove.

"Sorry about that," he said. "Would you like some sausage."

They ate sausages and drank cups of strong coffee that Sara brewed in the high-end machine on the counter. It had been a gift to her father from one of his clients. Thinking of her dad made her want to cry, but her eyes were too sore, too fragile from yesterday's emotional onslaught to allow for that. She breathed deeply and resisted giving in.

As they drove to Sara's doctor appointment, they made a list of items needed at the grocery store. Sara had taken her father's expensive pen out of his desk drawer and was now making notes on a legal pad she had brought along.

"I'll cook dinner tonight," said Sara. "I'm not much better than you, but I have been doing it quite a little bit lately."

Dudley stopped the Mercedes at a red light. He turned to Sara as if surprised by something.

"I just thought of something," he said, "we don't have any money. I mean, I have a little left from what I brought with me, but not nearly enough to go clothes shopping. Angelica's been paying for everything with a credit card."

"Just stop and get the credit card," said Sara. "Dad's office is almost directly on the way, anyway."

When John pulled into the lot, he parked in a slot reserved for visitors.

"Why don't you park in dad's space?" asked Sara.

Dudley shrugged as he got out of the car.

"You coming?" he asked.

She shook her head.

Moments later, when he had returned to the car and headed out toward her appointment, he passed on Angelica's *hello and best wishes* to Sara.

"She really wanted to see you, but she completely understands. She knows that all of this is probably a little overwhelming at this point."

"She's a nice woman," said Sara. "She took very good care of my father for as long as I can remember."

"Well, anyway, we're rich," said Dudley. "She gave me a credit card."

As he steered into the lot of the medical center where Sara's appointment was scheduled, he spoke without looking at her.

"Would you like me to come in with you, or would you prefer that I wait in the car?"

"I don't have my insurance card or anything," she said in a panic. "What if they don't even see me?"

She ran her hands through her hair and then slapped them down hard on her thighs. Clearly agitated, she began to cry.

"It's alright, Sara," said John. "Pei Ling and Angelica took care of all that. Just relax, Sara. Let's just get through this one thing, okay? Then we can go get something to eat."

"Why don't you wait in the car," she said as she opened her door. "I'll be fine. What's the doctor's name?"

Dudley began to worry after an hour. He thought of going in but knew that this could be crossing some line of trust with Sara. He attempted to think himself out of concern. Afterall, Sara had not seen a doctor, at least to his knowledge, in well over a year. There were things to check with a young woman. Things he didn't know about nor wish to think of.

She returned to the car just before one and sat loudly in her seat.

"Everything good?" he asked as he started the car.

"She asked me if I had entertained any thoughts of going back to the farm," said Sara.

"That sounds crazy," said Dudley.

"Apparently not," said Sara. "Apparently it happens all the time."

"I hope you won't give that any thought," he said.

She sat silently for a moment.

"Am I married?" she asked.

"I'm not sure," he said. "Different religions have different interpretations of being married. In some Native American cultures all you have to do is say that you're married, and you are. Did anyone marry you?"

"He did," said Sara without looking away from the windshield.

"Was there a license of any kind?"

She shook her head.

"You're no more married to that man than you are to me," said John Dudley. "Don't give any of that another thought."

John and Sara had selected a good day to visit the shopping mall. It was a weekday, and the area schools were not scheduled to close for the Summer for another month.

Their first stop was the food court. It was now early afternoon, and Dudley was painfully aware that he had not eaten since the sausages earlier that morning.

"I always have a devil of a time picking what I want in these places. So many options," he said.

"I'm getting some pizza," said Sara. "I haven't had pizza since I was at Barrow."

They ordered three giant slices of pepperoni pizza and a basket of breadsticks. When Dudley had finished his first slice, he offered to share the remaining portion with Sara.

"I'm stuffed," she said. "But thank you."

When they had finished their lunch and had taken the paper plates and plastic silverware to a trash container, they headed into the central part of the mall.

"We should get a map of where all the stores are," said Dudley.

"Don't need it," said Sara. "I've been coming to this mall with my friends since I was a little girl. I know where everything is."

Bobo's was an upscale, trendy clothing store that catered to young women who could afford to look the way they wanted to look. The store was not large, and the selection of clothes was not expansive by any means, but it was the first destination on Sara's mental list.

Two pairs of jeans, three pairs of khaki shorts, seven tops and a variety of bras and panties later, and they were headed back toward the food court. Despite John's offer to help, Sara carried a bag in each hand.

"I want to stop at the sporting goods place," she said. "We go right by it on the way to the car. I need a swimming suit and a new pair of running shoes."

She wondered what had become of the french fry swimsuit Pei Ling had given her. So many tiny pieces of her life had slipped away without her noticing. This made her think of her father, and she quickened the pace as she and Dudley marched along.

She tried on three suits and selected a green and gold one-piece. She also selected a pair of very expensive running shoes.

"I'm going to wear these," she told the clerk as John was paying.

They walked back through the food court and were exiting the mall when Sara stopped and looked at John Dudley.

"Do you use the pool?" she asked.

"No. I haven't."

"You can, you know. I mean, you have to treat the house like you live in it, John. You should use the pool."

"It's cold," he said. "I checked it with my hand."

"It has a heater," said Sara. "I'm going to set it at eighty when we get back. You should swim."

They were standing in the lot only feet from the door.

"I don't know how," said Dudley.

Sara tilted her head.

"You don't know how to swim?"

He shook his head.

"Never learned," he said. "I fell off a dock at a lake when I was little, and it frightened me. I just never got back in, that's all."

Sara turned back to the entrance of the shopping mall.

"Come with me," she said. "I taught swimming to kids one Summer. We need to get you a swimming suit."

Dudley humored her by attempting to learn to swim. He wanted to spend as much time observing her as possible but did not want to make this obvious. The lessons provided a good opportunity to do this. He worried that, for all intents and purposes, he had been charged with her protection and, in a very real sense, her recovery. When he thought of his past, of helping so many people through crises, spiritual and otherwise, he suspected he might be in the right place at precisely the right time. But there was always the image of the little boy he had chosen not to help. He had been a coward, and this was something he would never be again.

"Alright, John. Hold on to the edge and kick your feet out behind you."

This was not as simple for John Dudley as it perhaps should have been. One, he was not what anyone would call a person blessed with agility. Two, he had a genuine, stomach-constricting fear of drowning.

"That's good," said Sara, although she had seen children younger than five perform the same exercise with greater ease.

She was standing beside him in water up to her waist as he attempted with only marginal success to remain horizontal. His swimming suit, a knee-length red and orange surfer model, had been selected for function more than fashion. It was the only suit on the rack that had a string-tie waist large enough to accommodate his mid-section.

"Now, try to put your face in the water and blow some bubbles while you're doing that," said Sara.

Dudley submerged his face in the pool and immediately came up choking and gasping for air. He had breathed in when he should have exhaled and was now coughing uncontrollably. His stomach, just above the level of the water where he was standing, was heaving up and down with each cough.

Sara knew not to laugh, and she didn't. Dudley saw this as kindness, but he also saw it as a moment of light. For that one instant, when Sara was forced to swallow her smile, she was out of the dark.

"Let's try again, John," she said. "You're doing really well."

Dudley heard the dish break from the living room. And he heard Sara scream immediately afterward.

"I'm sorry. I'm sorry. I'm sorry."

These words left her mouth more as a shriek than an articulation.

Dudley dropped the book he had been reading and moved quickly to the kitchen. Sara had been loading their dinner dishes into the dishwasher and had dropped one. She stood with her hands in front of her chest. Her shoulders were climbing and falling with each sob; she wrung her hands together.

"God, I'm so sorry," she said again.

Dudley stood beside her. She could not look at him. And it was in that instant that he grasped, fully and painfully, what she had been through. She would have been punished for breaking the dish, and he knew this. Despite moments of sunshine that crept without notice into Sara's world, much darkness remained. And John Dudley knew that his self-appointed job of seeing this young woman back to some sort of normalcy would take time. But he had time.

"It's okay, Sara," he whispered.

He wanted to touch her shoulder but knew this would be a mistake.

"It's a dish. You're home now. We have lots of dishes. It's okay."

She composed her breathing and wiped her cheek with the back of her hand.

"He used to make us pray if we did something bad. Mandy and I used to have to pray for forgiveness. Then he would have sex with us. Then we might get locked in the shed or in the outhouse."

"You're home now," said Dudley.

"I don't know if I can do it," she said. "I don't know if I can get all the stuff…all the shit out of my head."

"You can," said Dudley, "and you must. We're going to do it together. You need to teach me to swim."

Sara and John Dudley stopped counting days and then weeks. Once a week, they met Pei Ling for dinner, usually at the Italian restaurant that had been Dobro's favorite. On occasion, when Angelica had called and asked John Dudley if he could meet with one or another of the agency's clients who had become enamored of being represented by a former priest, Sara and John Dudley would drive to the office in Santa Monica. Sara would sit at Angelica's desk and talk softly about her father while Dudley would sit in Dobro's office and listen understandingly to the concerns of this actor or that musician. He always dressed in black for these occasions.

"I'll drive today, if that's alright with you," said Sara on a brilliantly sunny morning.

They were leaving the house in Topanga and heading to Sara's weekly counseling session, to be followed by lunch at a deli with Angelica.

"Let me get my crash helmet," said Dudley as he flipped her the keys.

A few miles into the trip Sara stopped at a red light.

"You know, he stole my car," she said, turning to look at her passenger. "That was my father's car, and he just took it."

"He got a car. You have you," said Dudley.

"That's very Zen, John," she said as the light turned green.

That afternoon, after they had completed their errands and returned to the house in Topanga, Sara sat in a lounge chair on the deck. She had gone for a long swim and now sat reading a book of Sufi poetry that John had given her. She had grown to enjoy many of these writings on self-contemplation, on love, on kindness, and John had been happy to make suggestions. Many religions, many cultures. They often talked about them over dinner.

Dudley had joined her and was standing in the shallow end of the pool, the waterline just beneath his rather substantial waist. He wore a pair of swimming goggles that barely fit his large head.

The sound of splashing caused Sara to look up from her book. Dudley was moving slowly from one end of the pool to the other. The stroke he employed seemed to combine the ease and grace of an overweight housecat tossed into the deep end and the sleekness of an arthritic sea turtle. He barely moved as he dog-paddled frantically towards the far end of the pool. He was exerting great effort to maintain momentum and to remain afloat, but it was working. After several seconds of herculean effort, he touched the far edge of the pool and turned back towards Sara.

She was looking at him. She wasn't smiling, but the air around her seemed ever-so-slightly lighter and more easily breathed.

AUTHOR'S NOTE

This is a work of fiction. All of the characters are of my creation, although I hope I have breathed sufficient life into them so as to make them real.

I gave some thought to having Paul Danko visit the farm one last time, but it seemed that there had been enough suffering for one story. He had other things to do; other hands to shake.

A brief note of thanks to Ellen Benoit for creating my website. Please visit if you are so inclined. Feedback of any kind is always welcomed and truly appreciated.

frankdeweystaley.com

IIII III IIIIIIII IIIIIIIIIIIIIIIIII IIIIIIIIIIII IIIIIIIIIIII I III III

Printed in the United States
by Baker & Taylor Publisher Services